The Proposal Game

A Scorched Continent Novella

MEGAN E O'KEEFE

Copyright © 2018 Megan E. O'Keefe
All rights reserved.

ALSO BY MEGAN E O'KEEFE
www.meganokeefe.com

The Scorched Continent Trilogy

Steal the Sky

Break the Chains

Inherit the Flame

PART ONE

1

Lady Halva Erst sat on the balcony of her father's home, and catalogued all the things which were wrong with her lover. At the top of her journal's blank page she scrawled his name: Cranston Wels. Seeing no reasonable spot in which to embellish the letters of his moniker, she drew a scrolling vine of ivy beneath.

"Where to begin?" she asked.

"He has a weak chin," Silka offered.

Halva eyed her dearest companion through the slashed shade of the frondleaf canopy. Silka wore snug leggings beneath her high-slit skirts, in the martial style, and a drab brown top without any sleeves or ornamentation at all. A fashion transgression Halva supposed she got away with due to the popularity of the exiled commodore, Thratia, who had recently taken up residence within the city. One's fashion transgressions often became strokes of genius, when one wielded as much power as Thratia.

Silka thrust her sewing needle into a stretched silk canvas, thread tangling as she attempted to drag it through the fine, delicate cloth. Halva bit her tongue, nipping back advice. Though Silka's mother was desperate for her only daughter to be more ladylike, Silka had always appeared allergic to all of the softer arts.

"His chin is quite scholarly. It alludes to a gentle soul." Halva waved her pen, brushing away Silka's concern.

Silka pricked her finger with the needle and hissed at it. "Fine. He's too quiet when he speaks, I can scarcely hear a word he says."

"That is the mark of a confident man. A man who knows that his words are worth hearing, and doesn't need to yell them out to be heard."

"His height, then. He's far too short. You wouldn't be able to wear the latest heels from Valathea while on his arm, you'd tower over him." She held up the hoop. "Does this look like a bird to you?"

"A bird's nest, perhaps." Halva slumped into the soft netting of her chair and let her pen lay idle against the pad. "A man of his height saves on cloth, and my feet grow sore in those high shoes anyway."

THE PROPOSAL GAME

Silka stabbed away at the embroidery hoop, looking more like she was attempting to skewer an annoying insect than stitching the delicate petals of a red cactus flower. Halva smiled. Silka was such a delight, even if she was terribly misguided on the dispositions of men.

"He has a stutter." Silka reposted.

"I find it charming."

"His sister is a bore."

"I wouldn't be marrying *her*."

Silka leaned forward and rested her forearms against her knees, the hoop dangling between loose fingers. "Halva, we both know what's wrong with him."

"He has no viable prospects," they said in unison, parodying her father's gruff voice, and had to stifle giggles least they be overheard.

Halva shifted to the side, draping her arms over the railing of the balcony. Her family's home stood on the fourth level of the tiered city of Aransa. A respectable neighborhood, if not as desirable as the second and third levels. From the balcony, the entire city splayed out below, cascading down the mountainside to the blazingly hot sands of the desert. Even at midday, when the sun's glare was full, the streets teemed with the bustle of life and commerce.

Aransa may have been a mere outpost of the Valathean Empire, but its proximity to a firemount with a rich selium mine made it a thriving one. Airships slithered through the clear skies, black dots bobbing along near the firemount which produced the selium gas that made flight possible.

"There must be hundreds of potential suitors in the city," Halva ventured.

"But you don't want them."

"No, I don't." She leaned back into her chair, folding her hands across her lap. "But I don't suppose that matters. Now that daddy is back from the southern reaches, I won't be able to carry on with Cranston. It's best I cut my losses now."

Silka narrowed her eyes. "The expedition was unsuccessful, wasn't it?"

An embarrassed flush crept across Halva's cheeks. "Of course it was. Daddy hasn't been able to sense even a whole ship full of selium, let alone a pocket hidden underground, since his brain-fever. I don't know why he insists on these expeditions—they're just draining our savings away. He hasn't found a new mine in years."

"So Cranston's true crime is not being a sel-sensitive." Silka stabbed her needle in the air as if spearing her point.

"Yes." Halva sighed and covered her face with her hands. "I don't want to marry a miner, Silka. Their lives are so short and dangerous. But diviners are so rare. If only there were another kind of selium-sensitive... If only Cranston *were*."

Silka tapped Cranston's name on the notebook with one scarred finger. "But what about your research? Your family won't need sensitives if it can transition industries. Your work with fruit-bearing succulents is phenomenal."

Halva paged back through her notebook, shutting away the name of her lover. She traced her fingers over the delicate blooms her own hand had drawn, the ink bold and sure. Mentally she ran through her notes, a series of successes and failures, in cross-breeding the rapid growth of Valathean vines with the hairy empress, the most drought-resistant of the fruiting cacti. A cacti which, unfortunately for her esteemed highness, bore small dimpled fruits the deep purple of the empress's formal vestments. And, naturally, were covered in soft, downy spines.

Halva had found her inspiration in her late mother's old gardening book, the pages filled with plants so strange to her eye that they may as well have been mythic. But one, a thistle vine, proved the spark to her imagination. It could be, the book had claimed, trained to climb up trellises to frame garden pathways with blossoms.

It had only taken her a single turning of the red moon to train her hairy empress to climb, and as she discouraged and stunted its limbs—withholding sunlight to push it upward—it began to blossom. Doubly beneficial, the plant could be taught to grow along an umbrella-shaped canopy to shelter its roots and keep the water in the soil longer, eliminating the plant's sense of drought conditions. When the plant bore fruit, they were large and juicy, laden with the nutrients that the plant no longer hoarded.

But Halva's family was a sel-divining family, and their concordant with Valathea would be dissolved if they dared branch into other forms of commerce. Without the imperial stipend, they'd be destitute in weeks.

"Halva?"

She started, not knowing how long she had been lost in the pages of her passions. "Sorry, it's just—"

"I know." Silka patted her knee. "Come on. Let's get your mind off of things. I heard there was a new ten tiles table down at the Blasted Rock." Silka eyed Halva's silk skirt and delicately embroidered blouse. "But you're going to have to change first."

2

Detan Honding, sole heir to the Honding family fortune, sprawled in a pile of half-rotten crates and cracked his elbow against an annoyingly hard rock. He gasped, and immediately regretted the effort. The air behind the Scrubwood public house smelled distinctly of the offings of its patrons. His throat spasmed, forcing a dry-retch that shook him down to the core.

Unfortunately for his already abused state of being, his dear friend Tibal was not far behind him.

"I said out!" The owner of the Scrubwood shouted, his reedy little voice echoing in the tight alley. Detan managed to roll to the side just in time to avoid being crushed by the airborne form of poor old Tibs. He crashed among the crates Detan had vacated, and Detan spared him a sour glance. It was just Tibs's luck that he'd come along and crushed the wood first, making a softer landing.

"Now, see here," Detan rasped as he hauled himself to his feet.

"I don't give a ratshit what you have to say." The owner hawked and spat. "Just clear out before I call the watch, understand?"

A familiar hand coiled about Detan's shoulder and hauled him back a half-step he hadn't known he'd taken. Tibs spoke before Detan could gather a retort. "We're shoving off now, no need to ring the watch's bell."

The proprietor glowered at them, fists clenching and unclenching to some unheard rhythm. Detan didn't need to know the tune to recognize when he'd been given marching orders. Affecting a calm stroll, he sauntered out of the alley and back into the bustle of the main thoroughfare.

With an indignant huff, he tugged his sleeves straight and shook detritus from his hair. Terribly rude of him.

"You did swindle him out of three bottles of his finest wine," Tibs said while plucking wood splinters from his trousers.

Detan eyed his companion. Standing a good half-head taller than Detan, Tibs's wiry frame appeared to be made of nothing more than the mast posts and thick canvas sails he tended. Tibs's hair was miraculously clean beneath the droop of a worn, grey leather hat, his already beady brown eyes screwed up tight against the glare of the sun.

"Well," Detan muttered, "It was rude of him to notice."

"Sure," Tibs drawled.

Detan rolled his eyes as he straightened his vest. Without the aid of a mirrored glass, he couldn't be certain, but he supposed he still looked fresh enough to venture into another establishment. There was only one suspicious stain on his sleeve from his tumble through the rubbish.

"Wish I had never stopped in this pits-cursed city," Detan said.

"If only you had remembered Dame Honding's birthday in any reasonable amount of time."

Detan cringed. The vision of his Auntie's slate-stern face rose within his mind, flinty brows cleaved down in disapproval. Sweet sands, but that woman was a war-axe. And also the only remaining blood relative that gave a toss about his sorry hide. Detan sighed.

Until he acquired an appropriate gift to make up not only for having missed her annual celebration, but for his time away and all the rumors he was sure had flitted back to her on selium-fueled wings, he could not return home. Where his money was.

And he could really, really use some money.

"We'll have to try once more, old chum."

"You can't possibly mean the Scrubwood again."

"No, no." Detan held his hands up in surrender. "I admit that particular excursion was poorly planned. I did, however, glean some small facet of information which might lead us toward a more fortuitous future."

Tibs eyed him so hard Detan thought the man's stare would crack his very bones. "Really. And just what might thata' been?"

Detan slung an affable arm around Tibs's shoulders and squeezed. "There's a new ten tiles table up at the Blasted Rock!"

Tibs sighed, but his feet started moving and they entered the stream of Aransan foot traffic, winding their way toward the level stairs. They'd found the Scrubwood on the twentieth level, a tumble-down sort of place that Detan had hoped would be perfect for their purposes. Now, he supposed, it was best to look up. And not only because he'd been thrown out on his backside.

That wine—he admitted to himself in silence—would have been paltry faire by his fine Auntie's standards. No. He should have gone up-level from the get-go. The proprietor of the Scrubwood had, he was certain, done them a rousing favor.

As they threaded their way through the thin foot traffic, Detan loosened the ties on his shirt and took to fanning himself with an open palm. He might have spent the vast majority of his life puttering around on the Scorched Continent, but the heat of Aransa was something else.

The city was founded along the side of an old mountain, its terraced levels reaching up from the desert floor to the peak. Directly across from the city, the great firemount rose, its conical mouth constantly wreathed with selium-lifted airships touring the mines or popping by for a refill.

But it was the stretch between the two mountains that caused the heat.

Black obsidian sand, the result of some ancient pyrotechnic dance he didn't dare imagine, reached between the city's mountain and its sister firemount. Beautiful by night, the sands were deadly come the day. Their bright, sharp faces caught and held the blaring rays of the sun. He'd even heard that Aransa would on occasion execute their condemned by forcing them to walk across that nightmare.

He cringed at the thought. At least his habits were more likely to land him in a jail cell than on the executioner's agenda.

As they crested the final span of steps to the eighth level, Tibs paused and cocked his head at Detan.

"You know you're terrible at ten tiles, don't you?" he said.

Detan grinned. "That's half the fun!"

He gave Tibs a hearty clap on the shoulder, and then scurried within the broad, welcoming doors of the Blasted Rock before his erstwhile companion could offer up any other protests.

3

Halva peered dubiously into the clay cup Silka handed her, trying to decide if the suspicious smudges around the rim were the effect of poor glazing or poorer sanitation. Oh, well. Halva tipped her head back and drank. At least she was quite certain alcohol cleaned most things.

Around her the patrons of the Blasted Rock went about their business; laughing and drinking and making under-table deals. Not a one of them let their dust-crusted eyes linger on Halva, which eased her nerves. Despite Silka's best efforts, she still looked the part of an uppercrust girl. The poorest jute-woven dress in all the Scorched couldn't hide the shine to her hair or the lack of sun-lines about her eyes.

So far as she was concerned, they could all keep on minding their own business. Her business, now, was to dull the pain in her heart with the rather sharp contents of her filthy cup.

"Stuff's strong." Silka leaned toward her across their little table and raised both brows. "Go slow, eh?"

Halva rolled her eyes. "Yes, mother."

Silka grimaced and sat back, her sharp gaze roaming over the denizens for the evening. The Blasted Rock was precisely what Halva had expected from a downcrust bar. Its patrons were dirty in a way that suggested the grime was baked into the fine lines of their skin, yet their clothes were well mended and many wore expressions sharp with ambition. Only a few desolate souls hung their heads over their cups, hair obscuring whatever troubled expressions they wore.

The tables toward the back of the room were the closest to anything like lively. There the ten tiles players sat, doing their best to make the Blasted Rock's new board look old and worn as quickly as possible. Cheers and groans lifted in tandem as small fortunes exchanged hands. Halva locked gazes with Silka and pointed her chin toward the players.

"Isn't that what you wanted to come here for?"

Silka snorted. "Not now. No one would want to be my match while that idiot is still willing to empty his pockets."

Halva squinted, looking for the foolish man Silka had marked. He was easy enough to pick out. Though his back was to her, those surrounding him wore wide, pleased grins. She scooted her chair back just a touch, tilting her head to get a better look at the table's designated loser.

His shoulders were rolled back, loose and open, and a thick clay cup sat by his elbow with lip-prints smeared all around its rim. The man's skin was dark as damp sand and roughed by the sun, his coat patched too many times to be of any value. He did not look the type of man capable of weathering such a loss. She frowned. Seedy as the Blasted Rock was, it wasn't such a rough place that the proprietor would allow a man too drunk to understand what he was doing to drain away all his money.

Halva shifted closer to Silka and whispered, "Do you think we should alert the Watch? Taking advantage of a feeble man in such a way is certainly a crime."

A crease marred Silka's brow. "I suppose he might be feeble-minded. He seems happy enough, and only a simple man could be pleased after having lost so much."

The man tipped his head back and laughed then, his hands disappearing beneath the table for a moment as he thumped his knees. As he leaned forward, shaking his head, his hair shifted and Halva stifled a sharp gasp. On the back of the man's neck, where a noble house's brand was worn, she saw the three stars of the Landed peek above his collar in white scar flesh. The crest above the stars she could not make out—but the stars were enough. Only three families had a right to claim ownership of land on the Scorched continent, the rest were all forced to pay parcel leases, and none of those three lived in Aransa.

With trembling fingers Halva set her cup down and leaned across the table until her lips were almost pressed right up against Silka's ears. "That man is Landed."

Silka let loose an undignified squawk. "Are you sure?"

"Look yourself," she hissed.

Silka pretended a casual glance the man's way, her eyes widening in shock. "Which one do you think he is?" she asked.

Halva pursed her lips together, considering. There weren't many Landed men too young for grey hair and yet old enough to be whittling their time away in a tumble-down tavern such as this. She *hmmed* to herself, tapping her fingers on the scarred tabletop.

The Rinston family was least likely, she decided. While they had men of the appropriate age amongst their ranks, they were insular and lived the furthest from Aransa—all the way on the northern shores of the Scorched—and spent most of their time vacationing back in Valathea. The Kaliads, perhaps, but they were far too obsessed with appearances for any of their number to turn up in public with grease in their hair and patches on their elbows.

That left the Hondings, the first of the Landed. But they were small in number, their male members all either too young or old—except... Halva's brows furrowed. The heir.

"Detan Honding," she whispered to Silka.

"Bah, could be any random bastard. Those Landed families drop trou more often than dancing girls."

Halva rolled her eyes, and endeavored to educate her friend on the finer points of noble politics. "Bastards may abound, but Dame Isla Honding brands only those she claims, and the Rinstons and Kaliads have taken her practice to heart."

Silka squinted at her, incredulous as always. "Are you sure? Thought the Kaliads hated the Hondings. Didn't Lord Kaliad set Isla Honding's dress on fire once?"

"Hate doesn't keep a family from adopting a good idea when they see one. And yes, I'm sure. I can't imagine who else. He's the right age, and is known to travel the continent on occasion."

"Because he's useless. Lost his common sense when he lost his sel-sense."

Halva rolled an indifferent shoulder. "He survived a rather tragic mining accident, or so the rumors say. I imagine that would break the mind of any man."

"And make him mad enough to lose his fortune at ten tiles?"

Halva grunted assent. "It does seem a bit much."

Silka touched her fingertips lightly to Halva's arm. "He's being watched by more than us."

Halva followed Silka's slight head tilt to spy a spindly man sitting in the back of the tavern, a table and a tankard all to himself, his broad-brimmed hat doing a poor job of hiding a roving gaze that alighted upon Detan more often than not.

"A bodyguard?" Halva whispered.

"They're usually cleaner."

"So are Lords."

Together they watched the Honding man for a while, pretending to be deep in private conversation while they sipped their drinks. It was not long before she grew to loathe him. His easy laugh rang throughout the tavern, bright and joyful, despite the fact he peddled away a smaller family's fortune.

That man—that glassy-eyed moron—was just the type of man Halva's daddy wanted her to marry. His birth was impeccable. Not only was he of a Landed line, but one that bore sensitives more often than not. He was orphaned, both of his parents lost to bonewither, and his matriarch aunt was said to adore him. Being no longer sensitive himself, he was free from Valathean-compelled selium work and his inheritance would no doubt see him into a comfortable dotage.

Of course, he was also a man renowned for his loose morals and lack of conviction. Lazy and, evidently, completely idiotic. Halva suspected that even her daddy would look past his gentle breeding to keep his girl away from a man who lacked the wherewithal to purchase a decent coat. Perfect on paper, terrible in reality.

She shook her head, then froze.

"Silka... I have an idea."

Halva drank deep the last of her nameless liquor, then stood and squared her shoulders.

4

Tibs tapped Detan on the shoulder, light enough not to disturb the hidden pocket of false grains sewn within his left sleeve. A tingle of relief plied its way through Detan's muscles—he was beginning to worry that Tibs would let him run with the thing long enough to get them both caught.

Not that Tibs was in any danger of being caught. He'd spent a pleasant evening sitting on the other side of the tavern, pretending for all he was worth he'd never seen Detan before in his life.

Affecting a tipsy sway, Detan turned around in his chair and squinted up at Tibs... Who was not Tibs at all. The light tap had belonged to a much lovelier face than Tibs could ever claim to have owned.

"My Lord Honding?" the woman said, raising delicate brows high to indicate the question.

He took her in, sweeping her from head to toe, using his feigned insobriety to cover the slowness of his wits. Did this woman know him? And if so—how? For all her soft smile and kind eyes, Detan was certain he'd never seen her before in his life. He'd remember her—she was too exquisite to be forgotten.

She had clearly put some thought into dressing down for this outing. And though her dress was plain in cut and fabric, the russet hue suited her tawny cheeks and tea-dark eyes well. She brushed shining mahogany curls from her shoulder and pursed her lips, impatience folding a crease between her brows.

"The skies above know how strongly I wish I was the lad you were looking for, my dear, but I'm afraid not. Name's Wenton. Wenton Dakfert." He tried out a smile, locking eyes with her while he pleaded in silence: *please don't push the matter, not now.*

"Forgive me, Mr. Dakfert. You have the look of... an old friend." Her small face lit up as she smiled, and she reached forward to slip her hand into his and give it a warm squeeze. Detan wasn't surprised at all to feel the scrap of paper she passed him.

"Think nothing of it, Lady. I hope you see your friend soon."

"As do I." She inclined her head to him and swept from the room, joining arms with another woman before exiting the Blasted Rock.

Detan turned back to his gambling companions and let loose a low whistle. Much to his relief, the others laughed. "Well now, that was the closest thing to luck I've had all day."

"Maybe your luck has turned," the dirt-crusted man to his left said. "Ready to try it out?"

The man gestured to the center of the ten tiles table, where wagers were to be placed in the square called the vault. Detan licked his lips, guessing at the weight of the real grains in his right sleeve. It was enough to see him and Tibs back to Hond Steading, his Auntie's home, in comfort if not style—but enough to purchase her a proper gift so that he could keep his head upon arrival? He couldn't be certain.

But if that woman had been a herald for the changing of his luck, then his head might very well be in danger at this table. Detan cleared a rasp from his throat.

"I fear the joy of it may have left me with the Lady's leaving." He stood as they groaned their disapproval. "I would wish you all luck, but I'm certain you don't need it."

The muttered complaints shifted into rueful chuckles. Detan took the opportunity to tip his hat—carefully, as to not cause the money secreted in his sleeve to jingle—and slip away.

Out on the street he ducked his head and shoved his hands in his pockets, his walk brisk but not urgent, his back stiff but not defensive. It was a special sort of saunter he'd practiced, and employed, many times. The kind of stride that could carry him from a scene without anyone who saw him finding him memorable enough to remark upon the direction he'd gone.

The meeting place he'd arranged with Tibs was a dingy little tea shop, down two levels and well back from any main thoroughfares. As he walked, he wondered at the lovely-faced woman and what she had meant approaching him in such a way. Clearly, at least to his eye, she didn't belong in a place like the Blasted Rock. And she had known it, too, or she wouldn't have put in the effort to conceal her station and yet, she'd dared to address him by title and name. Which mean what—exactly?

Detan scowled to himself, taking the steps down two at a time, no longer mindful of the jingling in his sleeves. Had she known he would be there, and waited for him? That didn't make much sense—he hadn't even known he'd be there himself until a scant half-mark before he'd walked in the door.

A chance meeting, then. He gnawed on his lip, letting the copper-tinged saliva of an abused mouth sharpen his mind. She had known him, his true name, but he was certain he'd never seen her before that moment. Nor her friend, for that matter, the militarily attired woman who had taken her arm as she left. Detan stopped short, and someone behind him cursed him for a sandblasted-idiot, but he scarcely heard the abuse.

The other woman had been dressed much in the same fashion as members of the Valathean Fleet... Did *she* know him? And if so, why not arrest him on the spot? Maybe she wasn't sure it was him, and had sent the pretty woman to try and trip him up—to make him show off by using his family name to impress her, and then the military woman could have moved in, sure of his identity, and made the arrest.

Detan growled to himself, feeling the fine grain of the thick paper in his hand. Whatever it was, it could at least wait until he had a good cup of tea in his hand.

The tea shop marked the end of a truncated alley, its mudbrick walls doing little to hold back the stifling heat. Detan pushed aside the curtained door and stood squinting in the gloom until his eyes adjusted. No proprietor greeted him, which was some small comfort. Detan had never had the patience for an overly chatty shopkeep. He liked to be the only fast-mouth in the room.

Pallet-wood tables and splintering chairs the proprietor had no doubt dug out of the backs of other alleys crowded the room. Detan wasn't surprised at all to find Tibs sitting already, a lopsided clay cup clutched between his tree-branch fingers. That old rat was never more pleased than when he beat Detan to the punch.

After giving the chair opposite Tibs a futile wipe, Detan sat and rested his forearms on the table. They clanged softly.

"How much?" Tibs asked.

"Enough to get us back to Hond Steading with full bellies."

Tibs's brows shot up. "And then you'll gift the Dame the treasure of your company?"

"I'll figure out something on the way." He waved a dismissive arm.

"You said that last time, and she kicked us out before I'd even gotten a bite of cake."

The proprietor arrived and sat the malformed twin of Tibs's cup on the table. Detan squinted at the dubiously thick, brown liquid and gave the air above it a hesitant sniff. Nothing smelled like rot, or poison, though it didn't smell particularly pleasant either. Detan handed the proprietor a half-copper grain and the man stomped off.

"We going to keep talking around it?" Tibs asked, covering his expression by taking a drink of tea. He didn't choke immediately, so Detan decided to give his own a taste—it was bitter and over-steeped, but still a balm to his dust-tired throat.

"I don't know who she is," Detan said.

"Her friend looked martial."

All the thoughts that had been rattling through his own tired mind surfaced. He shook his head to clear them and stuffed his hand into his pocket, digging around until he found the thick slip of paper. He laid it out on the table between them, smoothed away the creases with the side of his rough thumb.

A calling card. The cream-hued rectangle was edged with some vine or another, the blossoms all turning their sunny faces toward the name in the center. Lady Halva Erst. Detan blinked, shuffling through foggy memory. Nothing came immediately to mind.

"I don't know her," he insisted.

"Told you to grow your hair out," Tibs said.

Detan cringed, instinctively reaching back to rub his neck where his family's crest had been scarred into his flesh as a young man. The Scorched Continent was a wild place, and though its roots were ostensibly grounded in the traditions of their parent empire, the cities of the Scorched lacked a great deal of the social structure which made it impossible for impostors to move within society.

Here, more obvious measures were needed to sort the cream from the water. Family crests could be faked, of course, but the penalty for such a thing was always death—no appeals, no leniency.

"Erst... Erst..." Detan muttered to himself, something about that name tingling the far reaches of his memory.

"Diviners," Tibs said. "Historically, anyway. Don't know what good they've been doing lately. The Lord Erst had a brain-fever, rumor is he can't sense a buoyancy sack right in front of his nose. Just like you."

Detan cringed. "But I suppose his affliction is... real."

"I suppose so."

Tibs made a study of sipping his stone-cool tea, nothing but the usual wrinkles on his face.

Detan pitched his voice low, just in case the proprietor was lingering nearby. "Think she means to turn me in?"

"You are a grand ol' idiot, sirra."

"Her friend did look the lawful type."

Exhaling a weary sigh, Tibs leaned forward and fixed his beady brown eyes on Detan. He tapped the table with one finger, punctuating each point. "First—the Lady's not nearly connected enough to know about your little escape from a Valathean prison. That's not something the empire would share with just anyone, and news takes a snail's time in filtering from the Valathean archipelago to us down here on the Scorched."

"They mean to retake me—"

"Of course they do. Don't mean they want the whole of the Scorched knowing they've lost control of one measly noble brat, eh? They sure as shit don't want anyone knowing just what happened with your sel-sense. Second—the Lady's family is in decline, and though you yourself are not a prime example, you may have noticed that the Honding name carries a certain amount of respect."

"Just because we're Landed doesn't mean—"

"Yes. Yes it does. Your people *own* the land these people pay parcel leases on. Sure, the Hondings don't own Aransa, but Hond Steading is the biggest blasted settlement on the Scorched. Or haven't you noticed?"

"Ultimately it all belongs to the Empire," Detan protested.

"Sure, sure. But it's Dame Honding who has her hands on the reins."

"I don't see how—"

"Third—The Lady Halva Erst is unmarried."

"How could you possibly know—?"

"Sweet skies, sirra, she still calls herself *Erst*."

"Then..."

"Yes."

"Oh."

Detan stared into the murky depths of his tea. It fit—all of it—he was annoyed to discover. The Lady's subtle smile, the tilt of her head. Her friendliness had felt false to him at first, a cover for the trap she was no doubt planning to spring... But, no. There was no trap, unless one counted love as such. The gentle woman had just been attempting to flirt. With him.

He hadn't even bathed this week.

"Sweet skies," he muttered.

"I hardly understand it myself," Tibs agreed.

Detan swirled his cup, feeling the weight of the silver grains he'd switched for the tin-plated marbles in his other sleeve. It wouldn't be long until that particular deceit was discovered, and then they'd have to clear out of Aransa for a time. Maybe if they stayed upcrust, where the Ersts of the world moved through life, they could avoid stumbling across those they'd swindled. It'd drain their silver, but...

"Diviners, you said?"

"Yes."

"A good long line of them?"

"Quite long."

Families like that carried their history like a shield. Parlors filled with artifacts to prove their lineage, walls lined with maps and treaties and particularly groundbreaking trade agreements. All things his dear, sweet Auntie might take an interest in. She and her fellow ladies had spent the last three seasons tittering on about their adoration for historicals, and he knew she was always itching to wow her hangers-on with some new trinket of obscure provenance. Trinkets which could not be purchased, no matter how much gold he managed to peel away from the pockets of the unwary.

Detan ruminated, tipping his head to the side. Halva surely meant to use him to lift her family's name, he was certain she had no interest in him as a man aside from the scar on his neck. It would do no harm for him to meet with her. To see where her intentions lay—and what objects in her household might tickle the fancy of dear old Auntie Honding.

"I suppose," Detan said, "we had best seek rooms at a more agreeable address."

Tibs snorted. "I thought you might say that."

5

Silka squeezed her arm so hard Halva feared the blossom of a bruise. With nary a word of polite explanation, Silka hustled them up the streets of Aransa as if she feared murderers nipping at their heels. Halva's breath shortened, a stitch wormed its way into her side. With an annoyed grunt she stopped hard and wrenched Silka's grip away.

"Are you trying to tear my arm off?" Halva straightened her shirt and smoothed the rumples free.

"Are you out of your mind? You couldn't possibly be interested in Detan Honding! Cranston may have a weak chin, but *that* man is a complete disaster."

"His chin is *not* weak. And of course I'm not interested in Honding. Sweet skies, did you smell him?"

"*Everyone* could smell him." Silka threw her hands in the air. "Then why even approach him?"

Halva was unable to keep a small grin from traipsing across her lips. "Because, my dear friend, Cranston is away until next week. And as soon as Daddy meets the young Lord Honding, he will find him just as reprehensible as we have."

Understanding lit bright in Silka's eyes. "But he's perfect on paper."

"Forcing daddy to see the error in his... requirements."

"You're mad, my dear. But I do love it so."

Arm in arm they took up the walk back to Halva's home, though this time at a much more decent pace. The sun was fading by the time they reached her front step, and fearing remonstration from her mother for being out past the falling of the dark, Silka kissed Halva farewell and stole away once more. Halva watched her go, loping down the nearly empty street, and admired for the first time the practicality of her split skirt and tights. They seemed much easier attire to run in.

Halva laid her palm against the smooth, green-painted door of her home, not understanding the hesitation in her own feet. The ancestral shadow fell across her, twisting the shade of their door-awning into the deep purple of a bruise. She glanced up at the jute-woven cloth, noting the frayed edges and falling hems. She'd have to have that fixed—it wouldn't do to have their guests wait even a breath under the full light of the sun.

A traitorous little snort escaped her lips. Have it fixed. What was she thinking? More than likely she'd have to take a needle to it herself. Her family could afford no seamstress.

The door gave way beneath the press of her palm, and for one frightful thump of her heart she feared the leather-and-wood hinges had shattered from neglect. But no, it was just Daddy, his soft grey eyes a little wide with surprise, the pink flush of the high winds raised in his cheeks.

"Good evening, Daddy," Halva said.

"Young lady!" He gripped her firmly by the elbow and steered her back within the shelter of their home. "I was just about to call the watch and have them search you out. Where have you been? With that *Wels* boy?"

"He's not even in the city." She disentangled herself from him and stepped away to place her sun parasol in the stand by the door. Gritty dust accumulated in the small corner between the stand and the wall, the desert blown in. Halva pushed away a sigh and made a note to start dusting again in the morning. She'd only done it the day before, but with their maid let go to save on expense... Well.

"Then where?" he asked.

She blinked, realizing he was repeating himself to her. "Just out for a stroll with Silka. You know how she just can't sit still."

"The Yent girl? She's a bad influence on you, my dear."

Halva waved a dismissive hand, turning toward her room. "I would argue I'm a good influence on her."

Father's steps pattered behind her. "Darling, she's practically native. Her parents even gave her a Catari name."

"Oh pah, my own name isn't so Valathean—it only has one flavor of vowel. And anyway, it hardly matters."

"You should be making friends with women of prospect."

She pushed her bedroom door wide and stepped within, kicking off her grime-crusted walking shoes. The old things were nearly indistinguishable from beggar's slippers, but they molded to her feet and kept the sand out and her skin blister-free. "And what if all the women of prospect are only interested in friends of their own sort?"

Halva turned, fists on her hips, brows raised high in challenge—and immediately regretted it. Lord Erst took a full step back, his head turning to the side as if he'd been struck. It was impossible to tell if he were blushing or not. The winds that carried the Erst airship had by now left permanent pink kisses on his cheeks, but his eyes were lowered, his lips down-turned.

"I didn't mean—" she began.

"No." He cut her off, forcing a smile. "It's all right, little flower. You're right of course. This last expedition was less than profitable."

"How bad?"

"You needn't worry." He gave her his false smile, reached out to squeeze her arm. "Everything will be well."

By the pits it will! she wanted to scream. But, seeing the pain wrinkling the corners of her daddy's eyes, the subtle tremble at the edges of his lips, she withheld her chastisement, kept her poppet's smile in place.

"If..." She cleared a thorn from her throat, gathering her courage. "If you'd allow me, I could speak to Warden Faud about my cactus. If he found it a worthwhile investment for the Arasan economy, then—"

"No, my dear." His smile twisted away into a bleak line. "We Ersts are diviners, as our concordant says. If we raise suspicions that our full effort is not bent to that task, then... Then Valathea may not be so gentle with us."

She was unable to hide her scowl. "Gentle? They halve our stipend every year we don't discover another selium pocket! The review is in three months, daddy. *Three*. Do you think we will still afford the lease here after that?"

His expression contorted, fear of the truth warring with blind-stupid stubbornness. She'd heard all his protestations before—the empire didn't have to give them anything at all. At least the airship was owned, they could always move into it. But then they wouldn't be able to afford the crew—and Halva had never been allowed to fly a day in her life.

"You will go to your room and stay there until you're able to discuss this with a level-head," he snapped.

"I'm *in* my room!"

He threw his hands in the air and stormed off, bare feet thudding down the dusty hall.

So. That was how it was going, then. Bad enough that even the most circuitous of discussions drove him to hand-wringing frustration. Halva chewed her lip, wanting to scream. Wanting to slam the door and stomp around as he did, as if bleeding off her rage would offer some clarity. It wouldn't, it never did. It just made her angrier.

And then empty.

With a grunt of frustration she scooped up her journal in one hand and abandoned her room for their small family garden. Work, she hoped, might bring her some small measure of comfort. At the very least the plants would keep their mouths shut.

PART TWO

6

The Lady Erst was a fourth-level woman, and that meant Detan needed fourth-level accommodations. He scowled at the gilded lace trimming on the awning above his head, the thin veneer of gold glowing bright enough to mock the desert sun. "Oasis" was stitched into the front of the awning, decorative flowering vines embroidered all around it.

"Guess they couldn't afford the real thing," Tibs muttered.

Detan shrugged. "Not like they'd grow long out here. Maybe on the northern coast."

"You're stalling."

"Of course I am. Do you see the polish on those doorknobs? Wiped down after every touch—that's how you know they're going to rake you over a barrel."

"Not like it's our money."

"Still. Who in the bloody pits can afford to hire a man whose sole purpose is wiping down door knobs?"

Tibs gestured to a black-jacketed man lingering near the door, doing his best to look ready to serve without leering at them. "The valets wear gloves, sirra."

"Oh."

Detan flicked dust from his shoulder, which settled right back down, and strode on up to that sharp looking young man. "Got any rooms?" Detan asked.

The valet, skies bless him, hesitated only a second—and Detan guessed at the retort that might be bubbling behind his lips. Detan knew what he'd say, put in the same cursed spot, but the lad had been trained too well to give over to sharp impulses.

"The Oasis is never full to capacity, sir."

"Of course not." Detan grinned at the befuddled young man. "Wouldn't want the soft-fingers to have to hear their neighbors, eh?"

"No expense has been spared in the construction of the Oasis, sir, you will find all the rooms appropriately quiet no matter the number of our guests."

Detan jerked a thumb at Tibs. "Got a room to make him quiet?"

The poor lad blanched, but Tibs jumped to his rescue. "If you could point us the way, we'd be much obliged."

Emboldened by the sudden usefulness of his profession, the lad laid one white glove on that perfectly shiny knob of brass and opened the door wide.

Where any proper inn would have put a bar and its bottles, a great pool of water stood, bluer than any sky Detan'd ever flown in. He guessed it about six strides across, still as a summer morning, and clear as imperial glass. All around the pool patrons lounged. Young men and women in valet-black uniforms stood at the ready, fanning them with paper-and-wood fans. Not a one of those gathered spared more than a curled lip for the dirt-crusted men wandering into their midsts.

"Good evening, sirs." A woman with a complexion like candied honey smiled up at him. "Will you require rooms?"

He allowed himself a small grin, seeing the subtle tension in the straightness of her back, in the white knuckles wrapped around the registry book she clutched close to her chest.

"Indeed, miss." He intentionally under-guessed her age and bowed with something like courtly grace. He'd never been very good at a proper court bow, but at least he knew where he was supposed to put his hands. Tibs just bobbed forward at the waist like a hinge had gone loose in his hips.

"Wonderful." The woman beamed at him. "The Oasis offers some of the finest rooms in all Aransa."

She paused then, letting the knowledge settle down around Detan's ears as if he hadn't already known it. He had to give the woman some credit for her tact—she didn't outright demand to see their money first, but the implication was clear. With a long-tortured sigh, Detan freed one of the slim pouches sewn to the interior of his sleeve and weighed it in the palm of his hand. He probably looked bored to her, but in truth he was making certain he'd grabbed the right pouch. It wouldn't do to pay for these rooms with what was left of their false grains.

"This should cover us for a spell, shouldn't it?"

Though he hadn't offered it to her outright, she took the bag and felt the weight herself, completely nonplussed. Though the contents were enough to make up a low-leveled family's fortune, she must have handled similar sums every day.

She turned and walked away from him, money in hand.

"Um..." He reached after her, thought better of such a feeble gesture and decided to follow instead.

She lead him to the lobby's west wall, where Detan was quite relieved to spy a set of scales and a sloped ramp for testing the grains' smoothness. "Forgive me," she spoke over her shoulder as she emptied the pouch into the waiting cup at one end of the scale and began to count out the measures, "but there have been counterfeits in this area as of late."

"Counterfeits?" Detan had the good sense to look aghast, and did his best to ignore the weight of the tin-powder painted glass spheres tucked into his other sleeve. "How brazen!"

"In many ways the Scorched is only half-civilized." The woman affected an apologetic tone as she removed the weighed grains and set them at the top of the ramp. With a deft hand she lined them all up behind a wooden bumper, then lifted it up and watched as they glided down in unison to the bottom. Not an odd landing to be spotted between them.

Detan let out a breath he hadn't known he'd been holding. Valathean grains were reliable currency. One had to have a specially crafted crucible, sieve, and furnace to melt the precious metals down and then strain them into the water which froze them into perfect little spheres. Still, counterfeits weren't unheard of, and some were a mite harder to spot than his own painted marbles.

"What you have here is sufficient for a seven-day's stay on our second floor, meals included."

"Though I'm loathe to leave your company in a hurry, miss, I don't expect to require more than five days."

Her hand moved to count out the difference, but Detan covered her fingers with his own. "If you could be troubled to find ole' Tibs and I some clothes, a hot bath, and a bottle of something strong and smooth, we'd call it fair."

The woman's eyes sparked, counting the difference, estimating the weight destined for her own pockets. "I'd be happy to assist you both, sirs."

"Excellent!" He pulled his hands back and clapped.

"Now I just need a name for the registry." She flipped her book open and magicked up a pen from somewhere under the table.

"Detan Honding."

She didn't even blink. "And you, sir?"

"Tibal."

"Family of...?"

"Got none to speak of."

That gave her pause. After a moment's hesitation she ended his name with a long flourish on the "L", just to fill up the space where a family moniker would go.

7

Of all the houses on the fourth level of Aransa, Halva's late mother had insisted upon this one because of the garden. Most of the homes around them boasted front sitting areas, manicured beds of multi-hued stones arranged in designs pleasing to the eye. Some even kept window boxes out front, stuffed full with succulents chosen not for beauty, but for flavoring food and easing sun-sickness.

The Erst family home, however, had been built by something of an eccentric.

His name was lost to her, though no doubt it was recorded in some imperial records room or another, but his love of the vegetation of Valathea remained. The house stood on the edge of the level, driving up its worth for the views of the city below, shoved as close to the street as he had been able to bribe the builders. Hence the single step up to their front door, while all other families tucked their entrances behind swirling patterns of rock.

In the extra space behind the house he had built a wooden canopy, offering blessed shade to the plants he had managed to grow there. Most of the plants had been outright disasters—so many were imported straight from the imperial archipelago without a thought to their native needs—but Halva had found the soil rich, and the gardening tools plentiful.

It was, she supposed, only natural that the study of those flowers which had delighted her mother became Halva's passion. This night, at least, it was a balm to her nerves.

The succulent fruit she'd crafted thrived. It had crawled up the umbrella-trellis she'd devised and was fruiting for the third time this year. Marvelously quick even by Valathean standards, if the scant notes she'd gleaned from passing mercer ships could be relied upon.

She cradled one of the fruits in her palm, this one the closest to ripening. The skin was firm and rough, reminiscent of bark, but she knew from experience the flesh would be sweet, dense and crisp. In just a day or two this one and its siblings would be ready to pluck. Halva chewed her lip, considering for a scant moment bundling them all up and marching upcrust to knock on Warden Faud's door.

Father would die from the scandal.

"Halva, are you out here?"

She startled with guilt, his voice layering over her thoughts of him, and let the fruit hang free. "Here, Daddy," she called, hoping he wouldn't sense the embarrassment in her tone.

"There's a man here to see you, dear."

No hint of annoyance tinged his voice, no sour note of condemnation that a man should come calling at such a late hour. Curiosity drew her forward, wringing the dirt from her hands against the apron stuffed with tools laid over her long skirt.

Faint light filtered from the sitting room's open door into the garden, illuminating the familiar sharp silhouette of her father—and some other man. He was a head taller than her, his skin made dark by too much time under the glare of the sun. She would have guessed he worked the mines, but the fineness of his clothes told her it must be airships instead. A captain, perhaps. Against the chill of the desert night he wore a close-tailored jacket of midnight cloth, and his leather boots looked so new they nearly shined. He had a friendly enough smile, and hair the color of oversteeped tea swirled with honey.

She'd never seen him before in her life.

"Forgive me, sir, but are we acquainted?"

He gave her a little grin, and she found something childishly endearing in it. "I had hoped so. You did offer me your card." He extended her a crumpled slip of paper with her own name on it.

Halva caught herself gawping and cleared her throat. "Lord Honding?"

"At your service." He sketched an overly formal bow, tucking his hands in precisely the wrong place against the small of his back. "I've come to apologize for the poorness of our introduction earlier this evening. And, perhaps, to ask you to walk with me?"

Halva darted her gaze to father, who shrugged. "Lord Honding is a gentleman. I leave you in his hands." Father backed from the garden, offering her a delighted wink.

Her stomach twisted. Of course he'd be pleased. How could he not be, when the scoundrel cleaned up so well? He extended her his arm, and she looked upon it with a distasteful curl to her lip. "Mr. Dakfert, you do clean up surprisingly well."

He turned his outstretched arm inward, transforming the gesture into another poorly formed bow. "I felt it was my duty to present you with a better image, after having affronted you with my attire earlier this evening."

She allowed her brows to creep as high as the vining cactus beside her. "Really? Or is it that you wouldn't allow your Lordship to be seen with a lowly diviner's daughter in public, but a private calling to beg apology and cease rumor is perfectly acceptable?"

He withdrew a half-step, turning his cheek as if struck. "I came to ask you to walk out with me, not to stifle any gossip."

"Then why the assumed name?" She stepped after his retreat, thrusting her finger forward as if deflecting a riposte. "Your reputation is a known element, *my Lord*, it would have done your character no harm to be identified card-playing in a third rate tavern. You had no reason to snub me so."

His rueful grin, a genuinely abashed expression, smothered the coal of her anger. "I confess that I was hiding, but not from you. Do you honestly think those men would have sat down to play cards at a table with Lord Honding as willing as they had Mr. Dakfert?"

"I suppose not," she said. It was silly to keep punishing him so. She wanted his attentions—though not for any real romance. He was, she supposed, objectively attractive, but it was Cranston who held her heart. And despite his current comportment, it was this man who could make her dear Mr. Wels look like the better choice in comparison. If she could get him to reveal his contrary nature to her father. If. It seemed like a reasonable enough gamble.

"My Lady?" he prompted.

"I accept your explanation. Though if you were really working to hide your identity, you might have considered growing your hair out." Inwardly she cringed—those were not the most romantic of words. But he laughed anyway, and so far as she could tell his amusement was not feigned.

"Then may I ask an explanation of you?"

"You may."

"Why is it a lady such as yourself was drinking crinnit in a third-rate tavern?"

"Crinnit? Is that what that vile stuff is called?"

"I'm afraid so. And no, you don't want to know why."

She shivered. The root word *crin* was known to her—it was old Valathean for death—and nit, well, that was clear enough. Though she'd spent a fair amount of time experimenting with insecticides, she'd never expected to drink one. Forcing on a pleasant smile, she extended her hand to him. "I suppose I could be persuaded to tell you while we walked. Where did you have in mind?"

His gaze swept her, and she knew what he'd see. The same simple dress she'd worn at the tavern, her hair ruffled from lack of care, her dirt-smeared apron tucked with tools. Not exactly the look of a woman to be seen on any Honding's arm, but she'd seen him in much worse shape only a few marks ago. At least she smelled better. His gaze lingered on her tool belt and skimmed away, taking in the garden and her notebook left open on the worktable beside her. He nodded to himself.

"I should like to take you to the gardens on the first level."

"Those—" She cleared a hitch from her throat. "Those gardens require passes. Too many have been walking on the beds and stealing blossoms, so the Warden had to limit visitors. It's so late... The guards wouldn't let us in."

He rubbed the back of his neck. "I don't think that will be a problem."

8

Detan left the Lady Erst in the care of her father, dropping sweet words in her ear before stepping back out into the night. The fat moon was out and heavy, its crimson light casting the whole city in a rosy glow. It would be a while yet before its smaller, silvery sister joined it and started trouble. The monsoon season was still a good full moon-turn away.

The dear lady had proved most pleasant company, a not entirely unwelcomed surprise. It was, at least, a relief that she felt no compunction in telling him when he had behaved like an idiot. Tibs would probably welcome the help in sharing the burden of the task. He shook his head to clear it, paused to take in a deep draught of the bracing night-air.

Charming as she might be, he couldn't let her infer too much from his interest. He only meant to get close enough to see if there were something his dear Auntie might desire within the doors of the Erst estate.

Guilt threatened to raise its ugly little head in his heart, but he shunted it aside. Young Miss Halva had intimated that her family was in some sort of trouble with its concordant, and her father had seemed far too willing to place his darling girl in Detan's unworthy hands.

No, she was attempting to use him as brazenly as he was her. There was no other reason for her to have approached him at the tavern—even if she was in her cups.

"Mr. Dakfert," a man called.

Detan turned, just before he realized what a monumentally stupid thing it was to respond to the false name he'd given a bunch of cut-throats he'd been defrauding.

"Who?" he asked, lamely.

They detached themselves from the shadows, surprisingly light of foot for men he had seen stumbling-drunk earlier in the day. There were only three of the five he had played with, which might have been a comfort if Detan thought he could ever fight three men on a good day. He'd thought a lot of fool things in his lifetime, but never that.

"No sense playing that card now, I seen your face. Got a mind for 'em, I do." The speaker took to the center of the lane and advanced straight upon him. Detan recognized the man well enough, remembered the sight of his fingers—twisted, broken one too many times—playing cards with intense care. A man who'd had something worth losing, Detan had reckoned at the time. He wish he'd paid more attention to the man's knuckles than his cards.

The other two he hadn't thought much of, but then, when a man'd been swindled and had a leader to rally to, well, even the gentlest men were capable of following orders. They broke away and began to walk down either side of the street, fanning out to flank him. Detan walked backwards, gaze darting for any sign of the city watch. At least he'd stand a chance of talking his way out of trouble with them.

"You must have mistaken me for someone else," Detan said, just to keep the conversation flowing. "I've only just arrived in town. Perhaps if you describe this devil of a Mr. Dakfert, then I could assist you in locating him?"

A furtive glance over his shoulder showed the road opening up into a wider lane. Still empty, storefronts and residences all battened tight.

"I can describe him, all right, can't I boys?" A disturbing chorus of chuckles answered him. "He's 'bout ye height." The man raised his hand to the top of Detan's head. "Dark as a beer-shit. Got a mouth on him too, a good one for busting. Fond of *glass*."

"Fond of the stained window arts?"

"Not. Exactly."

The vise closed. Detan yelped and spun on his heel, meaning to bolt in any direction which seemed likely, but ran chest-first into the extended arm of one of the men. His breath left him in a violent rush. Gasping, he staggered back and turned, only to have his arm yanked around by the other.

Pain sparked stars behind his eyes and he jerked free, but fists he couldn't even identify landed upon his chest, his stomach, his back.

Warm blossoms erupted all over his torso and then he was curled around himself on the dirt road, choking in dust with gasps of air as he tried to make his body as small a target as possible.

Blind instinct rose in him and his senses expanded of their own will—searching, searching. Trying to find any tingling hint of selium nearby. Trying to do his own murderous trick once more. There wasn't any close enough for him to sense.

He was perversely glad of it.

The blows slowed, switched to fumbling hands clawing through his clothes, bleeding out what few grains he had taken with him to bribe any necessary guards. Popping off his stamped brass buttons, his carved-shell collar stays.

Detan lay panting, heart racing, stifling groans as their probing fingers nudged newly sore spots. Let them rob him—just so long as he lived. *Skies above, let me live.*

His leg twisted, and for one horrifying heartbeat he feared they were going to break him just for the joy of it. But then his ankle bent, lurched, and he almost laughed as he realized they were stealing his boots. Typical.

Hands pressed his side and he flinched, fearing more abuse, but instead they shoved him over. He lay on his back, staring up at the crimson-tinged stars, looking less rosy now and more smeared with blood. One of the bastards slapped him, hard, and he jerked back into something like alertness.

"Good," the speaker hissed. "Now listen up. This—" He shook the little pouch Detan had taken with him. "Ain't a quarter what we're owed."

"The boots alone are worth another quarter." He spat in the dust. Someone kicked him in the side, and he fell into a coughing fit. Fingers tangled in his hair and jerked his head back. A pitted face eclipsed the night.

"Saw you walking with the lady, neh? Don't know what shit angle you're playing her for, but here's a new one for you. You get us the rest, plus half again *interest*," he spoke that word as if it were foreign, "and we leave you to your business. You got three days. Otherwise, we ask the lady to pay. She can't—well, we'll just see then, won't we?"

"What's to stop me going to the Watch?" he snapped, then cursed himself an idiot.

Something clanged against his teeth—hard, round, tasting of briney tin. He sputtered, tried to spit it out but they crammed his jaw shut, pinched his nose. Panic overrode sense and he thrashed, but they pinned him down.

He strained, felt his cheeks purple, doing everything he could to push the little false grain up with his tongue to force it against his lips. To do anything but—he gulped, his chest spasming against his will, and sucked the ball right down.

Shuddering overtook him, his whole body working against his will to expel the obstruction. Searing pain lanced down his throat, his lungs burned, his eyes watered. He was jerked to his knees and flailed, trying to grip anything at all to brace himself against.

The hands came off his mouth and nose and he heaved, sputtering, gasping. Someone got their arms under his ribs and lifted, hard and sharp, and the blasted marble erupted from his airway, damn near shattering a tooth on the way out.

Detan collapsed, every sinew of his being giving up to false relief. The threat remained. But he had no strength left. Not that he could have done much at full tilt.

"You listening?"

Someone slapped his cheek and he jerked eyes he hadn't realized he'd closed open.

"Good. Stay conscious, now. There are people round here at night that will take advantage of a man while he's down."

They laughed and left him there, curled around his pain, nurturing indignity alongside agony. When their steps had trailed away he forced himself to his knees, to examine the damage. It wasn't as bad as he feared. They'd centered their attack upon his chest, his torso, striking hard enough to bruise deep but not so much as to damage organs. A professional touch.

Gingerly he brought his fingers to his face, but felt no pain there aside from the searing rasp of his throat. Of course. They wouldn't want to alert the lady that there was anything wrong.

With a groan he heaved himself to his feet, brushed dirt from his tattered clothes, and hobbled forward a few uncertain steps. It would be a long, long walk back to the Oasis.

Gods below, Tibs was going to be pissed.

9

Halva caught herself humming as she sat the still-hissing teapot on the table between her and Silka. Sharp sunlight broke over the city, chasing away the blushing glow of the moon with fierce golden light. The night's chill clung to the breeze, gentled by the rising day, and the air smelled sweet and fresh.

Silka, however, was giving her the stink eye.

"You seem awfully pleased with yourself," she said.

"Well, of course I am." Halva waved away her friend's raised brows and poured herself a cup. "My plan worked quite perfectly."

"Oh, has it now? Are you and Cranston happily engaged to be wed?"

Halva grimaced, but hid the expression beneath a sip. "Not yet, not yet. But the Lord Honding did come calling last night, and daddy doesn't appear to suspect a thing."

"Of course he doesn't. How could he, when your interest is so obvious?"

A cough took her and she nearly snorted searing tea. "Interest? You do me injury! It is all quite play-acting."

"Really? And where, perchance, did that lovely flower which adorns your hair come from?"

Her hand shot up and found the offending blossom, tucked behind her ear. Hoping the gesture appeared appropriately careless, she plucked it free and examined it as if seeing it for the first time. It was a lovely specimen, thick petals rich with a faint pink that the dear lord had said resembled her blush.

Halva cleared her throat. "This thing? A gift from him of course, though I must have forgotten it, I cared so little for it." She pitched it over the balcony, though the gesture pained her. A real specimen from the first-level gardens might have had something interesting to tell her upon dissection.

"You." Silka pointed with one hand as she scooped up her cup with the other. "Are besotted."

"I am no such thing!"

"Halva, dearest, please sit back down. Your fuss will draw your father's attention."

Biting her lip, Halva forced herself to sit and spent a moment smoothing her dressing robe. "Yes, well, he is charming enough, I grant you. But I am entirely in Cranston's thrall. I shan't need the lord's attentions much longer, anyway. I must be done with him before Cranston returns in, oh, five days, is it now?"

"You don't even know." Silka shot her a viperous grin. "It's not like you to lose track of the time."

"I am only uncertain because these mercer caravans are often waylaid."

Silka brushed away her friend's words and charged forth. "You may find his attentions difficult to shake, my dear. If you cannot bring your father around to see him for the scoundrel he is, then your plan is thwarted. What signs has he shown of his deviltry?"

Halva hesitated, twisting the edge of her robe between two fingers. "None as of yet, I admit. The blasted man must have discovered a bath and a tailor between the tavern and when he came calling. Daddy was quite happy to hand me over into his care."

"Now that is a problem." Silka tutted. "The man must be revealed as a scoundrel."

"I'm quite certain he will reveal himself in time, it's his nature. Whatever he thinks he's gaining here most certainly won't override the reality of who he is for much longer."

"And what benefit do you think he's after? What if the dreadful man truly desires to settle down here in Aransa?"

A sour flavor blossomed on Halva's tongue. "He wouldn't. A Landed man like him wouldn't harbor any real interest in an impoverished lady such as myself anyway."

Silka rolled a dismissive shoulder. "You never know. He is getting older. Maybe that iron-headed aunt of his has put the pressure on for him to settle down. He'd pick whoever he fancied. Money's not an issue for a man that wealthy."

"You think?"

"I have no idea—it's only speculation. But it is a risk you run in this game, becoming the Lady Honding."

A shiver ran through her. "We must find a way to discredit the man without drawing attention to myself."

Silka set her cup down and leaned forward, eyes roguishly bright. "I have just the idea."

"Oh?"

"We must set him up. For a theft.'"

"Silka! I don't want the man arrested, just socially embarrassed."

"Oh pah. He'd never allow himself to actually be thrown in the clink. The moment suspicion is raised he'll be halfway back to Hond Steading to hide under his aunt's skirts."

Halva pitched her voice to a conspiratorial whisper. "But what would he steal? We've no idea what the man's true interest in me is—yes, yes, I understand you think it may be real romanticism. But what if it's not? What if he has some other fiendish plot in mind?"

"We beat him to it." Silka snapped her fingers in revelation. "You're having him over for tea this evening, right?" Halva's head bobbed. "Perfect. Take him on a tour of the house—let him see everything, and try to discern where his interests lie. Jewels, art, that sort of thing. The man must have something he cherishes. Aside from young ladies."

Halva rolled her eyes. "But what if it's something we can't part with?"

"Then don't show him those things. Let him see only what you can do without."

She brought her tea back to her lips and sipped slowly while she considered Silka's plan. It was daring, but she had no trouble with that. Seamless, in a way, but something about it gave her pause. They were missing something, she was sure of it, but she couldn't needle out just what that might be. Silka popped a pastry into her mouth, shoving it to one side so that her cheek bulged while she ate. Halva smiled—she never could figure out why her friend chewed that way.

"All right," Halva said. "I'll do it. But if he won't steal the thing, then what?"

Silka grinned. "I'll take it, and we can both swear we saw him do it."

"Oh, that's nasty."

"Love's a serious game, my dear." Silka winked.

"We'll need witnesses on hand, respectable people who might just listen to two hysterical young ladies."

Silka snatched up a sweetcake and danced it through the air. "Throw a small party welcoming the Lord Honding to Aransa. He hasn't been properly introduced to society here yet."

"That sounds... expensive."

"Oh! I know, say the Lord's a delicacy chaser. Real lover of food. Everyone will want to contribute their own fare to the party in hopes of impressing a Honding. Maybe we can even get the Warden to pay his respects, and try one of your fruits...?"

"It's settled." Halva stood and tugged her robe tighter about her waist. "I'd better get started."

"Tea's a full handful of marks from now!"

Halva sighed. "I know. If I start dusting now, maybe the place will be presentable by then."

With a stern nod Silka sat her sweetcake down and stood. "Show me to the rags, my dear."

Arm in arm, they left the balcony for the sun to claim.

10

Thick, bitter liquid forced its way past his lips and Detan jerked awake, spluttering in the half-light of a shuttered lantern. Blinking through his sleep-swollen eyes, he rubbed the back of a hand across his lips and brought it away sticky. He scowled down at the brown smear, then at the room around him.

He was back at the Oasis, though he hadn't remembered the walk.

"He lives," Tibs said and raised his arms in mock celebration.

"Not by your graces." Detan worked up saliva to spit, then thought better of it when he saw the fine rug on the floor beneath his bed.

"Stop whining, this stuff is foul but it keeps the swelling down. You're so pulped about the middle I suspect you won't fit into those fine new pants of yours without it."

He forced arms trembling with weakness to push back the sheet laid over him and examined the midnight-hued landscape of his torso. The thugs had done expert work. The bruises centered in areas that wouldn't be shown by most clothes, and the damage was shallow enough that he wouldn't bleed out. A dead man was, he supposed, less likely to pay up. Detan examined his most tender areas with shaky fingers, flinching with every touch.

"How are my clothes?" he asked.

Tibs snorted and set the bottle of foul medicine down on the nightstand. "In better shape than you. Missing a few buttons and dirty, though. Our hostess took them to be cleaned and mended. You damn near made her faint when you came stumbling in last night. What happened? The lady not take kindly to you?"

"Halva was all sunshine and smiles, it was those thugs we had over at the Blasted Rock that found me out. Skies above, Tibs, I nearly... Well. I would have used my *sense* if it'd been available to me. Luckily there wasn't a drop of selium nearby."

Tibs waved away his concern. "There wasn't. And you didn't. Now get up and get yourself scrubbed into something like human shape. You've slept all through the blasted morning."

"Have I?" He grunted as he swung his legs off the bed. "Did I tell you the lady invited me for tea?"

"You did." Tibs rummaged through a wooden crate that looked rather crude compared to the rest of the furniture. "So I had some fresh clothes brought in for you until the others are mended."

He grinned as he yanked a dreadfully pea-green tunic from the crate and shook it out. "This was the best that could be brought on short notice."

"That is... monstrous."

"Suits you then. Now get on with it."

He hucked the tunic and Detan caught it with a grunt. "Such kindness. And what will you be doing while I'm at tea?"

Tibs grinned a toothy little grin. "Seeing about those new friends you've made, and what can be done about them."

He forced himself onto unsteady feet, took a breath that stung brighter than a hot poker, and began to hobble toward the washrooms. "No violence, you'd more 'n' likely crack your own skull open. You just make sure our cursed flier is ready to go when we need it. I don't want to get stuck on this rock a heartbeat longer than I have to be."

"Fine, fine." Tibs scowled and kicked the ground. "But I want you carrying this." He returned his attentions to the hideous crate and produced a thin leather bladder, its mouth tied tight and the strings at the end of either tie weighted by heavy clumps of lead. The bladder drifted through the air, no bigger than his fist, fighting against the weight at the end of those ties.

Detan swallowed. He didn't need to strain his senses to feel the selium constrained within that balloon. "Would look a mite funny, a man rumored to have lost his sel-sense walking around with some of it."

"I'm sure you'll think of some explanation. But for the moment, sirra, it's the only weapon you're any good with."

Gritting his teeth, Detan took the ties of the balloon between two fingers and held it out before him as if it were liable to burst into flame at any moment. He supposed that wasn't too far from reality.

"Seems drastic."

"If you'd had it last night, you'd be walking straight today."

"If I'd had it last night, I might very well be a smear on the road today."

Tibs shook his head. "Take it. Or we leave Aransa. Now."

"I..." Oh, that was tempting. He wasn't too entangled with Halva, they'd scarcely been seen in public together. He could skate off without a word, and Aransan society would just cluck their tongues and chalk it up to the behavior of those odd Hondings.

He remembered, bitter as his medicine, the sneer of those men in the night. They knew he'd gone to see Halva. They'd take their price from him—or from her. Detan'd never counted himself a particularly principled man, but he had his limits.

"Fine." He gripped the strings tighter. "But get that damned flier ready."

Tibs snapped a mocking salute.

Detan scowled to himself as he waddled off to the blessed steam of their private bath. At least the tunic Tibs had found was loose enough to hide the cursed little balloon.

PART THREE

11

Dusting be damned, Halva would not miss the afternoon watering of her garden treasures. The worst of the filth had been washed away, those trinkets which she kept closest to her heart secreted within drawers and whisked off of pedestals. In the end, she had left most of the Erst valuables out. What wouldn't she trade to be able to wed Cranston with father's blessing?

With care she drew water from the family's heavy clay cistern, filling it to the second etched line from the top in the glass pitcher. She noted the day and amounts in her notebook, then went about dampening roots.

A soft rustling caught her attention, past the hairy empress fruit-vines, toward the back wall which butted up against the edge of the fourth level. Halva frowned, fearing some foraging creature, and slipped off her walking slippers. She picked one up and crept forward, shoe poised to strike whatever vermin had wandered too close to her garden.

From between the thornbrush a very, very human muttering emerged. Halva froze, fire racing through her veins, heart pounding hard enough to set her lips trembling. Cry out, or...? Her body moved before her mind arrived at anything like a decision.

She leapt, angling herself so that the thorns of the brush wouldn't snag her, and brought her shoe across in a vicious swipe where she had heard the voice. Her wrist jarred as she struck true, numb spiderwebs racing down her arm. She was scarcely able to hang onto the shoe. A man cried out, the words meaningless to her, and she brought her arm up again for another strike.

"Hold!" The voice was familiar enough to make her hesitate, the toe of her shoe pointing at the blue skies.

"Who are you?" She forced herself to stand tall, pushed back her shoulders and deepened her voice. "If you do not show yourself in peace this instant I will screech to bring all of Aransa down upon you."

A soft chuckle grated against her nerves. "I hope there won't be need of that."

Halva took a frantic step back as the figure moved, parting the thorny arms of the brush with extreme care. A tall silhouette against the sharp light, it took her a moment to place him. She dropped the shoe. "Cranston?"

He smiled ruefully, and rubbed at his reddening cheek. "I suppose I deserved that."

"Yes, you did." She folded herself into his arms, trembling all over with evaporating nerves. "Just what on the Scorched were you thinking, sneaking around my garden?"

He squeezed her tight, nestling his cheek against her hair. He smelled of dust and air and warm, milled hardwood. "That I would surprise you?"

She snorted and stepped back, holding him at arm's length. "You mean, that you could avoid speaking with my father."

He grimaced, then winced as the expression moved his sore cheek. "The thought might have crossed my mind." She brushed still-trembling fingertips against the arc of his unharmed cheek, admiring the shy curl to his lips, the ruggish twist of his wavy hair. It had only been a handful of days, and yet his simple presence soothed her, burnished away the nervous clamor of her heart.

"I missed you," she murmured, fingers trailing to his lips.

From the open hallway door came the soft thump of someone knocking. "Oh! He's here. You must hide." Panic fluttered through her once more as she pushed and shoved, forcing Cranston back into the thornbrush.

"Hide? What—who's here?" he stammered.

"Please, I'll explain later!"

A worried frown cracked a line between his brows, but to her relief he acquiesced, hunkering down amongst the biting brush until she could scarcely tell where he had gone. Heart hammering, she hurried away from the spot as to not draw any undue attention his way, and attempted to straighten the ruffled bun of her hair. It was only when she had gotten halfway to the garden's proper entrance that she realized she'd forgotten her shoe.

Her father met her first, pausing to give her a strange glance, a curious glint in his pale grey eyes. Whatever suspicions he may have harbored he shuttered as he stepped aside to allow the Lord Honding to pass.

Detan wore a pale green tunic and bark-brown trousers, cut loose in the southern fashion. The casual intimacy of him appearing before her in such a relaxed style caused a faint blush to rise unbidden to her cheeks. There was something reserved about his movements—nerves, perhaps?—and he had the pale look of a man who'd gotten little sleep. But his smile was easy, even if his bow was unusually stiff.

"I hope my late arrival did not put you off my visit entirely." He glanced to her bare foot and grinned.

"Not at all, my Lord, I sometimes... endeavor to feel the spryness of the soil." She cringed inwardly, wishing she'd taken the time to think of a more believable excuse—or at least spared a moment to reclaim her slipper.

"Your attention to detail is most admirable. Please—" He gestured toward the table and chairs at the center of the garden. "May we sit a moment? I'm afraid I'm not quite myself."

THE PROPOSAL GAME

Cold sweat trickled between Halva's shoulder blades and threatened to break across her brow. "Oh? Are you unwell, my Lord? Come inside, I'll make you tea."

She stepped forward in an attempt to push him into the house with the mere force of her presence, but he had already moved to the side and laid a hand upon the back of a chair. That hand trembled.

"My Lord?" She threw a worried glance to father, whose face was drawn in pale confusion.

"Shall I call an apothik?" father asked.

"No," Detan spoke a little too fast, the word coming out sharp. "I just need to sit." He lowered himself with care into the seat, wincing as his weight settled. "I am quite embarrassed to admit that I was robbed last night on my way back to the Oasis."

"Robbed!" Halva could not tell which voice carried deeper outrage—hers or father's. She put aside fears of the poor, battered man spotting Cranston and crossed to him, kneeling down to take a good long look in his soft eyes. They were bloodshot, but the pupils appeared to dilate well and tracked the finger she held up before them.

He smiled, and reached out to catch her hand in his. "I am whole, I promise you. My manservant is quite accomplished in these things. It's only... I may have rushed myself too much to reach your door this afternoon."

She smiled despite herself, and patted the hand that clasped hers with the other. "What happened?"

"Oh." He waved his free hand dismissively. "Low-level sorts, just picking on a man out alone wearing a nice coat." He sighed. "I was fond of that garment."

"Did they take much, my Lord?" father asked.

"Aside from my dignity, only some walking around grains. Nothing substantial. I daresay they were rather upset with me for having so little. Probably incensed them to the beating—ah, forgive me, Lady. You do not need to hear such ghastly things."

Halva stood and squeezed his hand. "I would beat them myself if they were here now."

"Halva!" father snapped.

"Well, it's true." She tossed a bit of hair that had fallen from her bun off of her shoulder. "I cannot believe the Warden allows ruffians to travel so high in the levels. What good are the stair guards if they can all be bribed with a bottle? But nevermind that. Here, let me fetch you some tea."

His grip tightened about her fingers, halting her turn away. "I would speak with you a moment, if I may?"

"Speak, speak," father said, waving them away with both hands. "I'll see to the tea."

Before Halva could protest, Detan pulled her down into the chair beside him. There was something serious about his gaze, unsettling enough to force her to pay attention, though her mind kept wandering to Cranston crouched in the thornbrush. The intensity, she felt, went beyond his upset at having recently suffered a beating. This was something else.

Her throat went dry as he leaned forward, nearly pressing his lips to her ear as he spoke. "Halva, I had not meant to do this, but I find I must tell you—"

"Remove your hands from her!" Cranston fought his way through the brush, tearing both skin and cloth on the hooked thorns. Halva bolted upright, thunked her head against Detan's in the process and let loose a rather unladylike curse. Detan was quick to follow her and—skies bless him—immediately stood between her and what was, to him, an unknown intruder.

"Who in the pits are you?" Detan's voice was rough with anger, but otherwise calm. His hand drifted toward the overlap of his tunic above his pants. Halva's heart leapt with fear as she realized he was reaching for a weapon.

"Peace," she blurted, grabbing his hands to keep him from producing whatever tool of violence he had secreted. "I know this man, he means me no harm."

"Blasted skies!" Father stormed into the garden. "Must you sour every aspect of my daughter's life?"

"This, this *scoundrel* was whispering against her ear!" Cranston thrust his finger Detan's way.

She summoned her courage. "It isn't what—"

"You don't have to answer to him, my dear," father said. "This 'scoundrel' is a gentleman. And one is prone to whisper against an ear when they are asking for another's hand in marriage!"

All three blurted, "Marriage!?"

"But I—" Detan paused to look down at her. His expression was bright, bewildered, his brows knit together with honest confusion. "We've known each other such a short time. I can't imagine—well. I mean, would you really?"

Unable to help herself, she laughed a little at his bemused expression. But before she could speak, father said, "Well, answer the man, Halva!"

Her feet rooted to the spot, her hands dampened with nerves. Father stared at her with wide-eyed excitement, clearly having misunderstood Detan's question. He'd only meant—well, she knew it was simple curiosity. But if she refused outright, she had no doubt he would disappear from her life.

No welcoming party. No chance to out him for the scoundrel he was in front of father. And no possible meeting with Warden Faud.

She chewed her lip, wrung her fingers together. Cranston's gaze bore into her side like a hot iron, she dared not look at him. Instead she stared hard at Detan. His expression shifted from bewilderment, to shock, to a hint of fear. He parted his lips, closed them, then parted them again. She had to do something—anything—to keep him from clearing the air. From politely excusing himself from her home, no doubt forever.

Cranston would understand. She would just have to explain it to him later.

"I—uh, I will?"

"You would?" Detan sputtered, still not quite understanding.

"What?" Cranston's voice was so cracked with anger and sadness that Halva's shoulders drew down in shame.

"Marvelous!" Father bounded forward and wrapped both her and Honding in his arms.

Whatever father said next, she could not hear over the sound of Cranston slamming the door on his way out.

12

"Walk me through it again," Tibs said.

They stood across the street from the station house of the Aransan watch, huddled in the shadow of a tenement building. Detan fluttered his hands through the air in a noncommittal gesture, unwilling to take his eyes from the yellowstone building across from them.

"It's quite simple, Tibs. I'm engaged to be married. Wedded bliss, matrimonial delights, that sort of thing."

"I understand the condition, sirra. It's the how of it, and the why exactly, that feels quite beyond my reckoning."

"Must you always be such an inquisitor?"

"In this instance I believe it's called for."

"Well, I could hardly say no to the Lady, could I?"

"Then she asked you?"

"Not precisely..."

"Then you asked her?"

"Certainly not!" Detan scowled at the raised brows of his friend and drew his fingers through his hair. "Her father quite misunderstood me, and rather insisted his daughter answer the question I *had not asked*. Why she said yes, I can only imagine. But the fact is she did, old chum, and so here we are. I could hardly tell her I hadn't meant to ask for her hand after she'd agreed to the thing. I'd have been thrown right out on my backside, and I hadn't even gotten the chance to explore the place yet. It's not my fault my mannerisms were misinterpreted."

"Your mannerisms?"

"I may have drawn close to the Lady so as to intimate that our thug friends may also be a threat to her."

"Drawn *close*? Really?" Tibs's eyes narrowed in suspicion. "Fine, we're stuck with it for now. But why in the blue skies are we going to the watch? I'm not keen on throwing myself in a cell, though you're welcome to."

"Protective measures, you see. The dear lady is in a tizzy about throwing the largest engagement party Aransa has ever seen. I've no doubt that our rough little friends will catch word of the thing and come to pay us a visit during the festivities in an effort to extort further gains from us."

"And you're certain of this because...?"

"It's what I would do." He grinned and slung an arm around Tibs's shoulders, marching him towards the station house door. "But if we beg for defense from the watch, then they wouldn't dare move against us, or her, so publicly."

"And what makes you think the rusted old watch-captain will believe you? Last time we blew through Aransa Captain Ganner threatened to hang us by our toenails."

"Because, old chum. Aransa has a new Watch-captain."

Detan pressed a palm against the heavy wooden door and swung it inward on well-oiled hinges. He squinted against the low light of the lanterns, blinking in the stone-chilled air. The door opened upon the station's central waiting room, but Detan hardly recognized it at first glance.

Someone had removed the mangy old rugs that used to line the floors and seen to it the tightly fitted rock had been swept clean. The entire perimeter of the room was ringed in bright lanterns, and although their light could never compete with the brilliance of the desert sun, they did an admirable job of chasing away the gloom.

A long, wide desk stood against the back wall, an alert young man in watcher blues standing straight as a mast pole behind it. Tables and chairs had been brought into the center of the room, and many held watchers and citizens alike going over local business.

It was all so very neat and modern that it made Detan's head spin.

"This... Might not be a good change for us," Tibs murmured.

A suspiciously cheerful looking woman approached them, her uniform coat pressed nice and crisp. "May I help you?" she asked, and Detan was a little startled to hear a friendly lilt to her words.

Detan forced himself to smile right back at her. "I've come to speak with the new watch-captain."

"New? Oh, you must have been out of Aransa for quite some time. Captain Leshe has been our guiding light for years now. What is it you wish to see her about?"

Leaning forward, Detan pitched his voice to a soft whisper. "I've come to report a mugging."

The blasted girl chuckled. "I'm afraid the Captain doesn't have much time for simple theft." She half-turned and gestured to an empty table. "If you two would have a seat, I'll send a watcher over as quickly as possible."

"Now, see here..." Detan hesitated, not quite certain what would win the woman to his side. "I'm sure you're all very good at whatever it is you do, but it's the Captain herself I need."

"I assure you that any of our watchers is more than capable—"

"I also have an invitation for her."

"Sir?"

He waved a hand through the air, suppressing a flinch as Tibs's heel dug into the top of his foot. "For a wedding. My wedding. I mean to say, my engagement party."

Her eyes narrowed just a touch which, Detan decided, was well enough. If she grew suspicious enough of him she just might call the Captain over anyway. "If you are indeed friends with the Captain, then I suggest you offer your invitation after her daily work is done. Now please sit, and I will fetch someone for you. What is your name?"

"Detan Honding." He plastered on what he felt was a rather triumphant grin, but the girl didn't even blink. She scrawled his name on the bottom of the list as if he were any other random piece of rabble.

"Someone will be *right* with you, Mr. Honding."

"Lord—" he began, but she had already walked out of earshot.

"Real nice," Tibs said as they took seats at the table the young watcher had indicated. "And here I was thinking you weren't trying to get locked up."

"This is disgraceful, is what it is. Time was when any poor soul could wander right into the station house and meet with the watch-captain. Most would have to pay a bribe to get back out again, sure, but this is ludicrous. Insanity. What sort of Captain makes herself unreachable?"

"One who's actually doing her job and doesn't have time for nonsense?"

"I'd like to think so," a woman said somewhere behind Detan's head. He was rather annoyed with himself for flinching.

Pasting on another pleased grin, Detan slid out of the chair and swung around to face the voice. She was lean of frame and tall enough to stand eye to eye with him. Sure enough, she wore the decorated jacket of a watch-captain, the little tin pins and crisp ribbons dangling from her epaulettes declaring she'd been captain three years and a deputy two years before that. Young for her post—and a rapid rise. Detan wondered if that meant she were competent, or the daughter of someone wealthy. In one hand she carried a thick envelope stuffed full with dog-eared papers, the other hung empty by her weapons belt.

"Hullo," he said, pretending ignorance. "Are you our assigned watcher?"

Her smile was simple, and predatory. He couldn't help but notice an awful mess of scars over her knuckles. "I'm quite certain you know precisely who I am."

"I, uh—"

"Captain Ripka Leshe." She inclined her head to him. "And you are Lord Detan Honding, so this must be your traveling companion Tibal…?"

"Just Tibal," Tibs said.

"So you say." She tapped the folder against her thigh. "You rather agitated my assistant. I wonder whatever for?"

"It was not my intention, of course," he said. The corner of her lip twitched—a suppressed smirk?—and Detan found himself wondering if maybe he'd bitten off more than he could chew in rattling her cage. "But violent robberies do tend to stir the blood."

"A violent robbery? Is this something you're planning?"

"Planning? Hah! No, it is something that's already happened—*to me*. I was beaten senseless in the middle of the street on the fourth level. The fourth! I was just a bare few steps from the doors of the fine Oasis."

"And did you know your attackers?"

THE PROPOSAL GAME

Her question, so sincere and apt, rocked him back a half-step. He took a breath and gathered himself. "I do not associate with the likes of robbers."

"Lord Honding," she spoke slowly, stepping forward to lay the folder on the table. It had his name printed on the front in a neat, familiar hand. The old Watch-captain's records, then. "I feel I must let you in on a little secret. I do, in fact, know all about you. About your cons and your games, about your history in this city. Such things make it very difficult for me to believe you are completely without fault in this case."

He licked his lips. "Captain Ganner had a grudge against me, I'll grant you, but this was an honest-to-skies robbery. Well, honest on *my* end, I wouldn't make any claims regarding the truthfulness of my assailants."

"They did him some real harm, Captain," Tibs said as he reached over and tugged the hem of Detan's shirt up just enough to reveal the deepening bruises beneath.

Captain Leshe's lips pursed in real disgust at the sight of his abuse. "I am sorry that someone in my city has done you harm. Be that as it may—"

"Wait, wait." Detan stuck both his hands out and patted the air. "Regardless of what you think of me, I have been attempting to turn over a fresh leaf. Lady Halva Erst, an upstanding member of your own city, has accepted my hand in marriage and I will not be denigrated like this."

"Congratulations on your nuptials." She smiled. "I hope you do not intend to live here in Aransa."

"Now wait just a moment, Captain, this city is her home and I—"

"And you, I must kindly ask to leave." She sighed once, shaking her head. "Though I suppose it would be fine to wait until after the marriage is complete. I wouldn't want to upset her father any more than necessary.

"And," she continued before he could pull himself together enough to protest, "Since I am, naturally, concerned for your well-being while you remain in my city, I will arrange a private watcher for you. One to follow you around at all times to be certain that you're not... robbed again."

"That hardly seems—"

"Are these all of the complaints you have to file with the watch today?" she asked, smiling that bright, sharp smile.

"Well, I suppose I'd like to file a complaint about being kicked out of the city."

"I'm sorry, Lord Honding. My decision is final." She picked the folder up, tucked it under one arm, and inclined her chin toward him. "Enjoy the rest of your stay. I expect you to be gone within a day of your wedding. If you are not, I will have you removed. Good afternoon."

She turned away and strode toward the back of the room, pausing only a moment to pass the folder she had carried off to another watcher.

"Well, that was terrible," Tibs muttered.

"Oh, stop it. At least we'll have a bodyguard now."

"You mean leash-keeper?"

"Same thing."

The man she'd handed the folder to flipped it open and skimmed a few pages, his brows drawing tighter together with each new line. Detan cringed. "Wonder what the old sod wrote about us." After a moment's thought over the possibilities, Detan whispered, "Come on, let's get out of here."

"Thought you wanted a bodyguard?"

"Sirs?" the watcher to whom Captain Leshe had passed the folder must have slipped up beside them while they were speaking, because Detan almost jumped out of his skin at the voice appearing over his shoulder. He was getting real sick of soft-stepping watchers.

"Well," Detan grumbled, "at least we know you're light of foot."

The watcher in question didn't look particularly stealthy. He was stood a good half-head taller than Detan, with shoulders wide enough to pull at the seams of his coat. "I'm sorry if I startled you, sir. My name is Banch Thent. I'll be seeing to your care during your stay in Aransa."

Banch's tone rolled right over the word "care" and for that Detan was grateful. He'd rather not have to deal with a smug watcher on top of it all.

"Well, Banch, I place my wellbeing in your capable hands."

"Thank you, sir. If you have no objections, I'd like to visit your rooms at the Oasis now to determine their defensibility."

Detan half-bowed and gestured toward the door. "After you, my good man."

The big bastard smiled indulgently. "You first, sirs. The rear is a more defensible position. Please attempt to stay no more than three strides ahead of me."

Detan caught himself grinning. Well, Ripka's watchdog had a brain somewhere in that thick skull after all. Trouble for him—it was always difficult to slip off when someone was keeping an eye on you from behind—but he could learn to work with that. He'd have to.

"I feel safer already!" Detan sauntered back out into the desert heat, ignoring Tibal's unamused eye roll. That old rock always took his sweet time when it came to seeing the fun in a good challenge.

13

"Is this your idea of a joke?" Silka's voice was hard and smooth as a riverstone, which meant Halva had really screwed up. They stood under the sparse shade of a reedpalm in Halva's garden, trusting the heat and vegetation to keep any would-be eavesdroppers at bay.

Silka shook the thick, folded sheet of paper at her and Halva flinched back. "I thought you'd find it amusing—"

"Amusing? Have you gone sun-mad? Skies above, Halvie, I do love you but—an engagement party? To *Detan Honding?* Do you have any idea what a tizzy my mother is in? You'd think someone told her I was liable to drop dead of old age at any moment. She's calling me an old maid now—bah! I wish I was an old maid!—but this little stunt of yours has put the wind up her. She'll have me married off to the first marginally acceptable man she can con into it!"

"She can't force you, you know, there are laws against that sort of thing."

Silka snorted and threw herself into a chair with a grunt. "There aren't any laws against guilting a woman to death. Or throwing her out on her backside."

"She wouldn't!"

"She most certainly would." Silka dragged her fingers through her hair and sighed. "My family doesn't even have a concordant to lose, and I haven't been able to secure an apprenticeship anywhere. It's either join the Air Fleet or marry well for me."

Guilt blossomed in Halva's heart, seeing the thin lines of distress spread from Silka's eyes and lips. Shunting aside her own worries, Halva pulled a chair close to her friend's side and sat, patting her knee. "You stop that now, it's not like you to mope."

"It's even less like me to get *married*."

"It won't come to that, not if you don't want it."

"The Fleet, then." Silka's lips pursed tight. "It's the only other way."

"I'm sure we can think of something. What about the watch? Have you inquired after a position there?"

"Sure, and so has every other hard-up soul in all Aransa. They're full up."

Halva scowled at the empty air somewhere over Silka's shoulder, letting her gaze unfocus as she dug through memory in search of an idea. The Fleet, she decided, would not do. Too often local joiners were shipped off into any old far-flung sector of the Scorched, where they spent their days chasing rumors of Catari uprisings and securing selium mines against bandits.

"You can't join the Fleet," she said.

Silka rolled her eyes. "I'd enjoy it, at least. The martial arts have always appealed to me."

"But they could send you *anywhere*."

"Traveling actually sounds nice."

"Without me?"

Her friend's grave expression melted under the force of her sudden, barked laugh. "It would be a terrible hardship, but we'd survive."

"You would. I'd wilt with sadness."

"Oh pah, you'll have Cranston's shoulder to weep on."

"If he ever forgives me. And anyway, it's not the same. He's not you."

Silka leaned forward, bright eyes narrowing with suspicion. "What do you mean, forgives you?"

Carefully restrained emotions threatened to bubble to the surface. Halva cleared her throat once, twice. Wrung her hands together in her lap and glanced around the garden to be doubly sure no curious ears lingered nearby. She took a slow breath, steadying the nervous buzz in her stomach, and leaned forward to whisper.

"He's here. He's back early."

"What?" Silka blurted loud enough to sting Halva's ear. She jerked back and looked around, heart racing until she was certain her father wasn't going to come stomping down the path.

"Shh, Silkie. I didn't know, and he, he tried to surprise me in the garden..."

"Here?"

"There." She gestured toward the thorn bushes which lined the back wall. "But then Honding came calling. Cranston hid, of course, and I did everything I could to distract Detan and father from the bushes and, well, I fear I did too much. The issue of marriage arose—"

"No! He heard?"

"Heard *everything*." Halva gathered her courage with a breath. "And came bursting from the shrubbery."

"Sweet skies," Silka murmured.

"Oh, he was livid. But I couldn't tell him just then, of course. You see, father brought Honding straight to the garden. He hadn't been given our special tour yet and I was afraid that if I spurned him I would never see him again. And I thought, well, if there was to be an engagement party for such an important man—"

"Then surely the Warden would come calling, and you could show him your research."

"I knew you'd understand! But Cranston, he was so furious..." She groaned and brought her hands up, pressing the heels of her palms against her eyes to still the ache growing behind them.

"I can't say I blame him. It must have been an awful shock." Silka reached out and squeezed Halva's intertwined hands. "But don't you worry, I'll have a word with him and get it all straightened out. We're going to have to move fast now, you know. This party—" She waved the offending invitation. "—is in two days. You might not have time to give Honding the tour."

"Then what? There must be something."

Silka winked. "We'll have to do his shopping for him."

"You have something in mind?"

"That depends. How committed are you to giving up the divining and going full over into horticulture?"

"Completely! I don't have the tiniest sliver of sel-sense, and neither does Cranston."

"Well then, we're just going to have to take the choice away from your dear daddy."

"You don't mean..."

"Yes, yes I do."

"The family atlas," they said in unison. Hope bloomed fresh and bright in Halva's heart.

14

Detan pressed his ear against the smooth, cold door of his room in the Oasis. Night fell across Aransa, and most of the hotel's guests had gone out to find food or other forms of succor. He should be out on Aransa's streets, getting all ready so that he might stand a chance of escaping the Lady Erst's affections, but he was stymied. The hall was silent as a windless dune, save for the intermittent steps of one Watcher Banch Thent.

"It's no good," Tibs said, "he won't abandon his post."

"A man has to piss sometime," Detan grumbled as he paced the edge of a small round rug in the center of the room. "It's not natural, the way he keeps on."

"Could be he already went and you missed it."

He stopped short. "You think?"

"Nope." Tibs licked his thumb and turned the page on his ragged book.

"Pits below, you're no help at *all*."

"Not trying to be."

Deten gave the overstuffed chair Tibs lounged on a kick, but the old rock-brain just grunted and kept on reading. Typical. Muttering expletives under his breath, Detan sat down hard on the edge of his bed and rested his forearms across his knees. He glared at the door.

"This is insufferable."

"Now you know what it's like being trapped with only you for company."

He rolled his eyes as he heaved himself back to his feet and stood a moment, trying to decide between pacing and listening at the door again.

"Argh," he said.

"Sweet sands, you are daft."

"Oh really, Tibs? And just what would you do about it?"

With an exaggerated sigh Tibs closed his book and laid it in his lap. "You can't shake the man."

"No..."

"So *use* him." Tibs brought the book back up.

"Huh." Detan propped his fists on his hips and stared at the door, rummaging up what he knew of the man standing on the other side. Young, ambitious. Eager to please his new Captain. Had a rather quick smile when it came to talk of the engagement. A romantic, then.

"Ohhh," Detan said.

"Finally." Tibs tucked the book back onto a shelf and pushed to his feet. Detan decided it would be rather charitable of him to ignore the exasperated tone of his old friend. Pulling straight the sweat-wrinkled collar of his ghastly tunic he reached out and swung the door open.

Watcher Banch blinked up at them from the soft candlelight of the hall, a little frown shuffling his brows into an arched caterpillar. "Is everything all right, sirs?"

"I'm afraid not." Detan sighed hard enough to make his shoulders slump and his lungs wheeze. "It's just that, you see, I would like to arrange a pleasant surprise for my dear bride. But, every time I work up the nerve to do it, I'm reminded of those brutes and I fear venturing out into the night."

The watcher's acute concern softened into the kind of worry often seen crinkling around grandmothers' eyes when they fear they haven't cooked quite enough food to feed everyone to death. "Maybe something could be arranged? I can call a runner-boy, if you'd like. The night market is bound to have something of interest."

"I fear no runner-boy can help me out of this spot, my dear man. You see, my darling girl—that's Halvie, of course—has intimated to me that she is dearlyfond of airships, but hasn't set foot on one since she was a little girl. It just so happens that my valet and I—"

"Mechanic," Tibs cut in.

"Yes, my mechanic and I, arrived in Aransa on a rather fine flier. I would so love to moor the thing close by so that I could take her on a jaunt after the party—a surprise, you understand. A little whisking-away. But I daren't brave the streets to reach the thing. It's currently stashed at a dock on the eleventh level, you see. It seemed a cheap and simple solution at the time, but now... Now I fear too much potential for peril lies between me and the old bird."

With a pained groan Detan slumped against the doorframe and leaned his head against it, watching Banch from the corner of half-lidded eyes. The young watcher pursed his lips and rolled them around, hooking his thumbs into the thick leather of his black belt. Considering, no doubt, how much harm could possibly come to them in the dead of night in levels as low as the eleventh.

"Well," Banch dragged the word out, "I suppose it would be all right. And anyway, you can't just abandon your flier down there." His eyes narrowed in mild suspicion. "Just what is the flier of Lord Honding doing so far downcrust?"

"We arrived at night," Detan supplied, having anticipated the question, "and so dropped the old bird as close to the night market as we could get. Dear Tibs's stomach was liable to crawl out through his teeth if we didn't find food, and fast."

The explanation was plausible enough. The eleventh was scattered with more rental docks than most, a loose confederation of those poor souls who either dreamed of working their way onto the big ships someday, or otherwise consigned themselves to a lifetime of garbage-shuttling and salvage-picking. The trash of Aransa was dumped by those brave spirits in a crevasse amongst the dunes—out of sight, and downwind.

The market itself was an oddity found only in the lower levels. While the uppercrust were able to do their browsing and purchasing during the day, those workers who toted the upcrust packages to and fro had to wait until the rise of the red moon to see about their own daily business. After certain hours, it was the only worthwhile place in the whole blasted city in which to acquire any kind of meal.

"Well," Banch said again, "let's get a move on then. I'm sure the Captain wouldn't want you parted from your rightful property."

Detan wasn't sure of any such thing, but he wasn't about to let Banch know that. Plastering on a delighted grin, he threw an arm around Banch's shoulders and ushered him forward, through the relatively safe walls of the Oasis. "Banch, my good man, you are a real treasure! An Aransan hero!"

Detan pretended not to hear it when Tibs snorted behind them.

By the time they reached the eleventh level, the night market was in full swing and the moon was at full rise. They bought honeyed millet cakes from a gap-toothed street vendor, and even Banch's fingers were sticky when they arrived at the docks.

The docking of airships in most Scorched cities was something of a pain. Keeping selium outside of the buoyancy sacks of the ships proved troublesome, as it was prone to escaping without the counterbalance of a heavy craft weighing it down. Many families chose to keep their crafts anchored close to home, tying them down to modified roofs and fences, but the unique nature of Aransa's stepped-level design allowed for another sort of arrangement: the edge of the levels themselves.

Docks sprouted all along the edge of the eleventh, protruding like crooked teeth over the twelfth. When the design had first been proposed, Detan had caught rumor of consternation by those caught beneath the overhang, but they soon withdrew their claims. After all, a constant source of shade could be a blessed comfort in the desert.

He skimmed his gaze over the hodgepodge of ships and dinghy's at rest in their stalls until he found his flier. The ship that served him as a better home than any well-made bed ever had wasn't much to look at, and he preferred it that way.

It was long and flat, maybe a dozen and a half long paces from end-to-end, crafted in the style of the old riverbarges with its sel-sacks ballooned up above it under thick rope netting. Though rectangular of body, Tibs had worked up a neat little pyramidal bowsprit to make it a hitch more aerodynamic, and Detan had made blasted sure that the pulley-and-fan contrivance of its navigational system was made of the best stuff he could afford. Or steal. Even its accordion-like stabilizing wings, folded in now, were webbed with leather supple and strong enough to make a fine Lady's gloves feel coarse and cheap.

Midship, just behind the steerage, rose a plain-walled cabin just wide and long enough to house two curtain-partitioned sleeping quarters. It was a good show for guests, but the real living space was hidden in the flat hold between deck and keel. Though the space was not quite tall enough for Detan to stand straight within, it ran the length of the whole ship—a sturdy little secret placed there by the smugglers who had originally built the thing.

"Ah, the sight of her is a balm against the sun," Detan murmured.

Banch smacked his lips. "Which one is she then?"

"There, the flat-bottomed flier without a name." He pointed as he hurried forward, the ticket-stub for his dock rental gripped tight within a fist he hid in his pocket. It had been a skies-blessed stroke of luck that the toughs who'd robbed him had missed it, otherwise those downcrust bastards might be toddling around the skies on his bird even now.

"Why doesn't she have a name?" Banch asked.

Tibs said, "Detan has enough trouble remembering his own."

All three shared a chuckle, though Detan and Tibs had been telling a variation of that joke at every other dock they put in at. Truth was, a name was something you could attach a story to. If they'd named the flier *The Bird* or some othersuch nonsense, then soon enough rumors would drift around the Scorched of the trouble people had whenever *The Bird* stopped for a visit. Wouldn't be long before dockmasters turned them away. He had a enough trouble already evading the rumors of the Lord Honding and his roguish tendencies. At least he could wave away any stories attached to his name as upcrust affectations. Stories that followed a ship, however, had a tendency to stick.

But unnamed fliers weren't uncommon, even if his was a bit big to be waddling around the sky without a moniker.

Detan handed the stall tab off to the wharver and the man lead them down the rows of ships. He paused before the flier and untied the single stretch of rope that blocked off entrance to the flier's gangway. The cheeky wharver gave them an elaborate bow, then spat over the edge of the level and trudged back to his post.

They scrambled onto the deck and cast off, Detan throwing the lines free while Tibs manned the complicated steerage podium covered in crankwheels and levers. Banch stood at Tibs's elbow, sticking close, his stance splayed just a touch too wide, knees bent as he adjusted to the subtle sway of flight. He was still munching on a millet cake, lips smacking, but Detan pushed the sound out of his mind.

Night breeze washed over him, and the nice Watcher was all unawares that this little surprise he was in the process of arranging was not for Lady Halva's benefit. No, if Detan had his way then the Lady wouldn't know that the flier was tied just beneath her garden's ledge until he was well on his way out of the city.

Detan sucked down a deep breath and bore his teeth at the moon. *Use him*. Hah.

The door to the cabin swung open, cheap hinges cracking in complaint. Detan spun in time to see Tibs leap to the side, slamming the gear-lock into place as he did so. The flier would not climb, sink, or turn until that lock was disengaged. From within the cabin two familiar brutes emerged. Each carried a heavy looking pry-bar. Detan doubted those tools had ever been used on wood. His stomach churned. They had, apparently, gotten a look at his stall tab after all.

"Our little friend came back early," one of the men said.

"Put down your weapons," Banch dropped his honeycake and yanked his baton out, sticky fingers white knuckled about the handle. "I am a watcher, and you two are under arrest."

The second man whistled low. "A real live watcher, eh? Good. Now we have someone official to *watch* us kick these two heads in."

They advanced, and Detan found himself sweating despite the bite of night.

15

"I told you I would find him, not bring you to him," Silka whispered. They crouched in an alleyway on the thirteenth level, hair and bodies hidden underneath old burlap tarps that Halva had once used to shade a few plants from the sting of the sun. It was the best she could do—not even Silka owned clothes plain enough to go without remark in this neighborhood.

"He should hear it from me," Halva said.

"I'm not even sure *seeing* you is a good idea. By the pits, darling, as much as he loves you he must also hate you right now."

"He wouldn't."

"You can't know."

Halva bit her lip to keep from saying something she'd regret. Silka was right, of course. There was no possible way for her to be certain about Cranston's state of mind and, if she were being truthful with herself, he had every right to hate her. She just didn't much like being truthful with herself. Not at this moment.

The door of the squalid little tavern they'd been watching swung open, spewing yet another of its guests out into the night. The man—or woman, Halva couldn't be sure—staggered down the gently sloping lane, spilling droplets from the mouth of the clay bottle they carried.

"Are you sure?" Halva asked again, sensing her friend tense in exasperation at her side. "I can't imagine he'd come to a place like this."

"I'm sure. Only his sister was at home, and she told me that their parents had put a hand on each shoulder and thrown him out for the trouble he was causing. Drunk, of course. She said he always comes here when their parents are tired of him."

"It's all so dismal."

"When you're getting drunk on the cheap you don't usually mind the decor."

Halva felt the sharp edge to Silka's tone and fell into silence. This was precisely the sort of lifestyle she was trying to avoid with her scheming. This, and winding up on the arm of some rich idiot she didn't—could never—love.

The door creaked open a second time and spit a familiar silhouette onto the street. Halva sucked air through her teeth so fast she whistled, then clenched her jaw to keep from crying out. Cranston staggered just as comically as the person who'd preceded him, but now that weaving walk felt tragic to her.

Swallowing the shame that welled up within her at the way she'd dismissed the earlier person, Halva straightened and adjusted the lay of the burlap wrapped around her. She needn't have bothered—she looked like a half-empty grain sack in it no matter what she attempted.

Exchanging a fortifying glance with Silka, she stepped out into the street. Then hesitated. Silka, skies bless her, strode on ahead, leaving Halva safely concealed in the shadow of the alley's maw.

Silka approached Cranston as if he were a frightened dog, one hand out and her chin tipped down. Halva couldn't hear what was said, but the tones were soft and smooth. After a moment, while Halva's stomach worked itself into knots, Silka pointed back toward the alley and Cranston looked up, peering into the darkness.

He staggered toward her. Nerves clamped her throat shut, and it was all she could do to keep from bolting back down the alley.

"Halvie?" he said.

"Oh Cranston, it's all just a terrible scheme. I didn't *mean* any of it," the words fell from her lips, all in a rush, jumbled up against one another so tight that she feared he wouldn't understand her. She squirmed, twisting the rough burlap between her fingers until it made her skin pink and raw. He squinted down at her, and she imagined she could hear his alcohol-addled mind working through everything she'd just said.

"I, uh, I know," he spoke with care, making certain not to slur his words. "It's all right, love. Silka told me everything." He grinned and held out his arms. "Everything's all right."

Tears she hadn't known she'd been holding back streaked down her cheeks, hot and salty. She folded herself against him, burying her face in the firm slope of his shoulder. He wrapped her up tight in his arms, and though he stank of sweat and fermented grains the embrace was still sweet.

"But you should go," he whispered against her ear, "your father will wonder if you're out so late."

"To the pits with him—"

"Hush, love." He brushed her hair, fingers a little clumsy and fumbling. "He means to do his best for you. When—" He cleared his throat. "When will this be over?"

"Tomorrow night." She made the words a promise with the force of them. "That's the engagement party. Warden Faud will come, and then.... Well. We'll see."

She felt his chin bump the top of her head as he nodded. "Silka will steal the atlas in Honding's name." His voice hardened with conviction. "I should be there. I should help her."

"Cranston, sweetie, father would never let you in the door."

He sighed so heavily he felt like a deflated buoyancy sack in her arms. "I know, I know, it's just..."

Halva chewed her lip as he trailed off. "Maybe Silka and I can work something out. If I distract daddy, then—"

He pressed a finger to her lips. "Focus on what you must do. Send Silka for me if you need help. I..." He cleared his throat and glanced away. "I'm sorry you've seen me like this."

She smiled and kissed his finger. It tasted of dry, fallow soil. "I'd be stupid-drunk too if our positions had been reversed. It's all right. I'll come to you the moment it's over. Goodnight, Cranston."

"Good night, Lady Erst."

He brushed his lips against her forehead and escaped her embrace, walking with just a little less stagger now as he turned up the winding lane. Up, back toward home. Halva's shoulders slumped with relief and she nearly fell as Silka put an arm around her waist.

Silka said, "It's not over yet."

"No, it isn't. But it's better."

They were not five steps down the road when a ragged creature stepped out before them. Halva stopped hard, heart racing. Silka took a half-step forward, reaching for something hidden amongst the folds of her burlap.

"Easy," the creature's voice was raspy but still distinctly feminine. "I'm not looking for a fight, Lady Erst. Silka Yent."

Halva's eyes narrowed. "Who are you?"

A sandpaper rasp escaped the woman's lips, "Just an old geezer who wants to wish you congratulations on your engagement to Lord Honding. The word's on the wind all over the city, miss. Not every day a Lordling like that ties hearts."

Giddy relief almost pushed a giggle through her lips, but she swallowed it down and forced a polite smile. "Thank you kindly, ma'am."

Silka angled herself to urge Halva onward, and she dipped her head to the woman in leave-taking.

"It's just a shame," the woman said, "that you have another lover. Wouldn't want the wedding to be called off, oh no, not with a match like that."

Bright embarrassment painted Halva's cheeks and she stopped mid-step. "What are you implying?" she snapped.

"Not implying any old thing, just stating a fact. 'Nother fact is, full mouths don't have much to say." She stuck a filthy hand out, palm up, and rubbed her fingertips together.

Revulsion swelled in Halva's belly. She'd brought no grains with her, hadn't even considered that she might need them. What a damned stupid thing to do. Swallowing her pride, she fumbled through her burlap wrapping in search of any likely piece of jewelry.

Silka said, "I've got a few—"

"No." Halva found the clasp of her bracelet and undid it. It was a simple piece, crafted of silver and real carnelian. A gift from father, brought back after his last successful excursion. There hadn't been any new gifts since then. "Here." She shoved the piece toward the woman's hooked fingers. "Take it and leave me be."

The woman snatched the bracelet and brought it close to her eyes, peering all along its length. No doubt she'd already assessed how much it was worth at the local pawn dealers. How much of whatever vice she favored she could get for it.

"A lovely start." The woman chortled and vanished the bracelet into her ragged clothes. "I'll be seeing you again soon, lovie."

Humming some delighted tune to herself, the wretched creature wandered away—down the lane—and left a chill deeper than the desert night behind her.

"What a monster." Silka broke the silence, fists clenching and unclenching at her sides. "Do you want me to go take it back?"

"No." Halva shook her head and pulled the burlap close, trying to ignore the sensation of her skin crawling. "No. Let her think she's secured something for herself. It's just one more day. Remember what we said? About what I wouldn't give?"

Silka's lips twisted in disapproval, but Halva ignored her. It was going to be okay. Cranston had said so.

Just one more day.

16

Detan was gratified to hear Tibs let out rather unmanly squawk as he danced out of the reach of one of the men's pry bars. Of the two attackers, one was considerably shorter than the other, and Detan was a little dismayed to see that one decide to take after Tibs. Great. That meant he had to deal with the taller of the two—and that piece of crusted leather looked meaner than a wet rockcat.

Detan was certain he really *hadn't* seen the man before. The shorter man he knew for one of his market-road attackers, the other's face was completely new, if not predictable with its scars and smears of dirt.

Wonderful. There were even more men out there wanting to crack his head than he had thought.

Banch let out a cry and sprung forward, putting himself between the tall man and Detan. For just a moment Detan stood there, feeling silly in his oversized tunic with his empty hands while all around a battle raged. Then he remembered himself.

Tibs had gotten a big, flat wrench in his hands and was doing an admirable job of knocking back the stocky bastard's swings, but he was losing ground fast. Yelling something even Detan didn't understand, Detan rushed across the deck and threw himself on the back of Tibs's attacker. The air thumped out of him as his chest collided with the man's back, cutting off his cry. Bright hot pain sparkled behind his eyes, all the bruises from the night before rearing their ugly little heads to remind him just how things had gone the last time he'd been stupid enough to get tangled in a fight.

He wrapped his arms around the big man's neck and held on for dear life, squeezing for all he was worth as the bastard swung his arms about.

"Pitsdamnit! Hurry up Tibs!"

Staggering to his feet—when had he fallen?—Tibs lurched forward and struck the man about the middle. The big man grunted, wheezing against the force of Detan's arms around his neck. He swayed a little, and Detan bore down with all his strength.

The world washed out from under him as the man collapsed. Detan let loose a mousey yelp as they slammed against the deck, all tangled up together, and in his scrambling to get away he just got tangled tighter.

"Hold still!" Tibs yelled.

"Banch! Help Banch!" Detan squeaked, trying to shake off Tibs's assistance while still worming to his feet.

"Easy," Banch said nearby, his voice soft as a man coaxing a startled goat. "That's all taken care of."

"Bloody skies." Detan let himself go limp. "Could have told me sooner."

"You were too busy screaming your fool head off," Tibs said as he got his hands underneath Detan's armpits and slung him back to his feet.

Detan stood and surveyed the damage. As far as he could tell, the flier was without injury. Sure, Banch was sprouting a red river from his nose and Tibs's cheek was swelling up like he'd kissed a scorpion, but the flier's smooth deck was unmarred save for a few red speckles, and the hinges on the cabin door seemed to have survived the abuse.

"By the pits." He grunted as a too-hard inhale of breath set his ribs creaking. "These bastards just won't give up."

Staunching his nose with a handkerchief, Banch knelt over the taller man and rolled him onto his back. The man was no more familiar to Detan unconscious than he was vital. Banch dutifully poked through the tough's pockets, finding little more than lint and a few stray pieces of twine. Banch scowled at this meager collection as if the force of a sour expression could transmute what he was actually seeing into what he wanted to see.

"Doesn't make much sense," he finally said. "There's nothing special about these boys. No club markers, if you get my meaning. They're just your usual street toughs. Better get them tied up anyway."

From a pouch at his hip he produced four well-worn sets of leather buckles and tossed two of them to Tibs, whom Detan had to admit was looking quite a bit more hale than his own sorry self. Under Banch's strict tutelage, they got the brutes trussed up sound, but not unsafely. Watcher Banch was, as it turned out, an education in the finer points of careful circulatory management of prisoners. Apparently the watch had experienced a rather damaging scandal when a blacked-out drunk slouched over his own knees while bound and ended up losing both his legs.

"Well." Banch brushed unseen dirt from his hands as he rose to his feet. "I had better check in the cabin to see what those two were up to."

Detan and Tibs exchanged a glance. "Help yourself," Detan said, and hoped the strain in his voice could be safely chocked up to physical exertion.

As Banch crept toward the door, truncheon held out just in case there should be a third interloper, Detan and Tibs slithered closer together behind him. They practically tip-toed as they followed him into the little cabin, with its thin cots and its flimsy curtained divider. Detan hissed through his teeth. The trapdoor was open. Those scuzzy bastards had been snooping around in his particulars.

"Stay here," Banch whispered without glancing back. He shifted to crawl down the ladder, and Detan caught the faint gleam of light from one of the oil-lamps below shining through the dark.

Over the subtle creaking of Banch's boots, Detan and Tibs held a conversation in eyebrows. Tibs, it seemed, was all for braining the poor watcher and being done with it. Detan didn't want innocent blood on his hands—especially not after meeting Ripka Leshe. And, truth be told, Tibs didn't want it either. He just liked to be contrary.

"Gentlemen." Banch's head appeared in the trapdoor's square of light. "What are you doing with this?"

He held up a few rough-woven sacks, their mouths and interiors sparkling like the topside of a dragonfly's wing. A few glass marbles clattered around in their bellies—the rejects the paint hadn't taken to. Their whole counterfeit operation, cradled in a watcher's hand. Banch's tone, firm and disappointed, made it clear the question was only a flimsy courtesy. He knew blasted well what he held.

"Would you believe I've never seen those before in my life?" Detan asked, forcing a grin.

"Not," Banch drawled, "for a second."

"Pity." Detan kicked the trapdoor shut and pulled the iron lock closed in one frantic motion.

Whatever Banch was shouting, Detan could scarcely hear it. The hull of their flier had been double-walled, the space between those two walls stuffed with wool. Detan slumped down until he sat on his heels, fingers tangled in the hair at the back of his head.

"Well," Tibs said, "I supposed you solved that problem."

"Oh, I'm sorry, did you have a better idea?"

"Not at the moment." Tibs turned around to look out the cabin door, back toward the two unconscious bodies slumped across the deck. "Looks like we've got ourselves a menagerie."

Detan forced himself to his feet with a rough groan. "I'm not about to get into the habit of taking in pets." He pushed past Tibs and kicked the boot of one downed man. "Certainly not *strays*. How do you think they found us?"

"We weren't exactly playing hard-to-follow."

"Didn't see a need for it."

"Saw wrong, then."

Detan paced the length of the deck, ignoring the ringing pain in his sides and chest with each step he took. "What time is it?" he asked.

Tibs glanced at the pale red moon—he'd always been better at telling the mark. "Four marks 'til sunup."

The stocky man Detan had choked into slumber groaned and shifted, fingers twitching. "We can't keep these two." He decided the moment the words had passed his lips. "We'll have to make a delivery on our way to the Lady's garden."

"And the Watcher?"

Detan grimaced, staring down at the reinforced deck as if he could see through it to the man no doubt pacing below. "He only had his truncheon, and the flier's a strong girl. He'll keep until the morning."

An unruly scowl twisted Tibs's lips. "If he damages the ship..."

"Then it might very well fall out of the sky. He knows that, the man's not a fool. There's water and food enough in there for a little while. Come on then." He pointed toward the steerage. "Let's get this fool course underway."

Tibs rolled his eyes. "If you say so. Sirra."

That title—Tibs's sirra—was enough to rake coals over Detan's spine. It meant, in the mechanic's humble way, that Detan was a colossal fuck-up. Which, he supposed, was completely fair.

Detan sighed and paced to the front of the flier while Tibs got it back under way. So much for using the watcher to their advantage. Now Detan had a hostage—one he hoped nobody found out about until he was safely on his way out of this cursed city. He gripped the deck-rail, knuckles going white. Four marks until sunup. Seven until his engagement party. He'd have to find some poor apothik still open at this unholy hour, someone willing to sell him something to keep his head up and his eyes open despite the fatigue and the pain.

Seven marks. And he still didn't know what he was going to pinch from sweet little Halva Erst. Still didn't even know what it was she wanted from him in truth. It wasn't marriage, she wasn't that mad. He sighed. When it came right down to it, Auntie Honding probably wouldn't even appreciate all the trouble he'd gone to to secure her gift.

PART FOUR

17

Half the families of the fourth through the second levels had come to celebrate the happy couple. Or, at least to see if Detan Honding was, in fact, putting down roots in Aransa. Halva had borrowed help from the neighbors—had the sitting rooms cleared of most of the furniture and a long table or two of local snacks laid out. Guilt gnawed at her. Even if things went perfectly to plan, the food was no small expense for her family to bear.

The guests seemed to be enjoying themselves well enough. She just wished Detan would hurry up and show already.

"Where is he?" she whispered to Silka, unable to keep the annoyed hiss from her voice. Silka beamed at the lady they had been talking to, some tanner's wife from the third, and wrapped vise-tight fingers around Halva's arm.

"Excuse us for a moment, won't you?" Silka didn't wait for the woman to respond before dragging Halva away from the sitting room and out into the garden. Where, annoyingly, no guests were mingling.

Silka released her and glanced around to be sure they were alone before speaking. "Blue skies, woman, you really must keep your voice down."

"I'm sorry, it's just—what if he doesn't show?"

"Then I'll find him and kick his head in."

A warbling laugh escaped her lips and she clapped both hands across her mouth to hide the sound. "I'm not sure that would help, Silkie dear."

"It would certainly help *me*."

Voices rose in greeting behind them, rowdy with delight. The kind of greeting appropriate to a freshly minted groom. Halva feared she might faint with relief. "Finally."

The party-goers clustered in the hall toward the front door, but they parted as soon as they spotted Halva coming. She sped her steps, hoping to intercept Detan before her father could reach him and implore him into some sort of ridiculous toast.

She stopped short when she saw who he had brought with him. It was not the young man at his side that gave her pause. Detan had warned her that he traveled with a gentleman friend who would join them in their celebrations. No, that young man was no surprise at all. It was the rag-swaddled woman and her nearly identical partner that caused Halva to dig her heels in and stare.

"Halvie!" Detan shook off the attentions of some mercer she didn't recognize and closed the space between them. His embrace was restrained, hesitant, and she returned it with equal care—mindful of the bashing those robbers had given him. Before he could get any ideas about their proximity, she deposited a kiss upon his cheek.

"Darling," she kept her voice low and soft, "who are your friends?"

"Ah!" He threw an arm their way and pointed to the well-dressed man. "That is my dear friend Tibal, and those fine young ladies—" He gestured toward the ragamuffins. "Say that you invited them, my dear."

"Do they now?"

The leader of the gaggle, a woman whose street-worn visage was familiar to Halva from the night before, bowed her head. "It was so very gracious of you, Lady Erst, to invite we downtrodden into your home to celebrate such a wonderful moment with you." Her gaze slithered to Honding. "I hope you haven't had a change of heart."

"No, no." Halva forced herself to offer her hands to the woman. They clasped hands, smiling at one another with all their teeth, and Halva felt the brush of her own bracelet against the side of her fingers. "I am just so delighted you're here. Please—" She pulled her hands back and motioned toward the sitting room. "Do help yourselves to some food."

The two trundled off, one of them giving Halva's waist a pinch as she passed by. Detan slipped an arm around her shoulders, warm and strangely reassuring, and ducked his head down to whisper by her ear, "Are you all right? You look as if you've seen a ghost."

"Fine—I'm fine." She forced a little smile up at him, reining in the urge to bolt off and find Silka.

Detan didn't look convinced in the slightest, but he mustered up a return smile and steered her toward the sitting room. As they passed a knot of uppercrust ladies, Halva heard a distinct whisper: "The Ersts really have taken a fall if they're entertaining *that* sort of company."

A spark of anger ignited in Halva's heart, her fists curling at her sides. From the corner of her eye she saw Detan's head turn toward the whisper, a frown creeping into the wrinkles at the edge of his mouth. Her anger shifted into fear. If he thought her destitute, he might abandon whatever his mad scheme was.

"I do find charity to be such a rewarding habit," she spoke quickly, head turned as if she were speaking to Detan, but her words loud enough for the group to hear.

His brows crept up in mild confusion, but then his sense of fun took over and he grinned. "Indeed. Dear old Auntie Honding can't stop raving about it. Charity is the perfect endeavor for any Lady of standing."

Halva smirked, she couldn't help it. No matter what tug-and-pull was happening between them, Detan had just socially devastated those women. By the end of the week Halva wouldn't be surprised if half the Ladies of the upcrust were giving over full marks out of their day in the spirit of charity.

Anything Dame Honding approved of was worth doing. Twice.

He winked at her, and she felt a traitorous little flutter. Blasted man. He wasn't the one she was interested in tonight. But he could certainly help her make headway with the one she had her eye on. Warden Faud had been stubbornly refusing all her invitations to the garden—too hot out, he claimed, while fanning reddened cheeks with a limp paper fan. But she had the Honding on her arm now—and if the reactions of those ladies were any indication, the word of a Honding could make people do strange things.

"This way," she said. "Let me introduce you to Warden Faud."

18

Silka lingered in the sweltering light of the Ersts' garden, their family atlas tucked under the hem of her shirt, and waited for Halva to corral the people she needed this way. It would only take a moment, a laugh at joke, her hand resting on Detan's arm, and then she'd have the atlas planted on him. He'd notice it, of course, the thing was blasted heavy, but she was convinced she could screech thief loud enough to drown out any protestations.

If only Halva could herd the man out here. A few witnesses couldn't hurt, either.

The crunch of feet on gravel drew her attention, and a jolt of recognition raced through her. A man walked toward her down the central path, looking much cleaner than the last time she'd seen him. He was taller than her—a rarity—and built like a clothesline. His attire was well tailored, his charcoal trousers and loose top cut to emphasize the lean muscle of his shoulders while allowing him easy movement. His boots were older, though, worn smooth. The boots of a man who didn't let you hear he was approaching unless he wanted you to.

"You were at the Blasted Rock," Silka said, just to see the look on his face. His smile was small, pleased. Controlled.

"I'll confess to that." He stopped two paces back and inclined his head. "And you were the Lady's martial friend."

She snorted. "Martial? Not yet."

"What do you mean?" He looked away from her, studying the plant by his side, giving her space to answer without scrutiny.

"I'm not as well positioned as Halva. It's marriage or the Fleet for me." Silka tried to keep her voice light, flippant in the face of her fate, but she heard it crack anyway.

"And you'd prefer the Fleet?" He brushed his fingers over the vine, glossy-dark leaves catching in the sun.

"What are you doing out here?" she snapped.

He shrugged. "Looking."

"You mean snooping? Casing the place, perhaps?"

Those narrow shoulders twitched, and she allowed herself a triumphant smile.

"Just observing," he said. "What are you doing out here?"

"Waiting."

"For the Fleet?"

Heat blotched her cheeks. She saw his gaze flicker, all the amusement leaving the lines around his eyes. Before she could tell him to leave, he said, "Sorry about that. I've been too long in singular company."

Silka glanced back toward the sitting room to make sure no one else was headed their way, then took a half-step forward. "What are you two up to? Really?"

"Would you believe," he drawled, "shopping for a birthday present?"

She snort-laughed. "You can't be serious."

He held his hands out to either side, palms open to the heavens. "Sirra Honding doesn't often know when to quit."

"And you?"

"I quit just once. Left the Fleet—honorably. Best blasted decision I ever made."

Silka's stomach knotted, the sudden seriousness of his tone wrenching up tight her already growing sense of dread. "Some of us don't have a choice."

"But we find ways, don't we?" He reached out once more and laid his hand against the vine. "You know what I've observed here?"

"I have a feeling you're going to tell me." She crossed her arms and arched a brow at him.

"Clever lass." He winked. "I've seen dust between the floorboards. Scrubbed down recently, sure, but if you don't keep it up on the regular it gets stuck in the cracks no matter what you do. The food's subpar for an upcrust family, the servants all borrowed from the neighbors. And, strangest of all, all the real valuables are tucked away—not out to be shown off."

"Inconvenient for you, you mean."

He chuckled. "Possibly. But also telling. The Ersts are in trouble. What, exactly, does Halva want with Honding?"

The amusement faded from his tone as he finished speaking, the words sharpening until they cut off, brittle with resentment. He didn't know. He had ideas, and she suspected they were good ones, but he didn't *know*, and it was killing him a little. Killing him to risk his friend in a situation he didn't understand all the variables of. Silka clutched the atlas against her belly with one arm.

"She wants a husband."

"But not," he said, "Detan."

"No."

"Ah. Interesting." He half-turned to the table tucked amongst the fruiting vines and flicked open the cover of the notebook that lay there.

"You can't possibly know the whole scheme," she protested.

"Lady, I've been doing this a long while now. It's not so difficult to puzzle through." He didn't take his eyes from the book. Silka leaned forward to watch his face as he shuffled through the pages, but couldn't tell just how much he understood of what he read.

"You can't take that," she said.

He blinked, startled, and turned away from the book to look at her.

"Wasn't considering it."

"I'll make you a deal," she spoke slowly, flicking her gaze from side to side to make sure she wasn't overheard. "I'll make sure you find something nice for your birthday gift, or whatever it is you really want, and you take me with you."

"Really." He looked her up and down, one brow raised. "And you mean for me to believe you *don't* want us to take something? So that Miss Halva can discredit Detan? Not that he needs the help, mind you."

"Here." She slipped the atlas from its hiding place and offered it to him, palms damp with fear or shame or anger—she couldn't tell. "Good faith. Take it."

"We don't need another set of hands, or another mouth." He took the atlas all the same, lips thinning as he turned it over in his hands. It was a singular piece of work—or so Halva had insisted, Silka didn't know much about such things—and as thick as her wrist was wide. Its pages were yellowed with age, but the ink within was still bright and crisp. Halva hadn't been the only botanist in her family's long history. The leaves and barks which were used to make that time-resilient ink still grew in Halva's garden.

"You mean to trade this for your freedom?" he said at last.

"If you'll let me."

A bulge appeared behind his lower lip, and she realized he was running his tongue over his gums as he thought. A little moth-wing's flutter of hope thrummed through her. He was considering. At the very least, even if he denied her her flight, she had that.

"You can't come with us."

The tremble of hope died, stilled. Turned to a cold lump in her chest, heavier than any pitted fruit. He paused, watching her above the pages he held out open before him still, waiting for her to speak her mind.

"Why?" was all she could manage.

"Because—" He tipped his head toward Halva's botany book. "Your friend's going to need help. You should be here for her."

"She won't be able to help *me*." The venom in her voice surprised her, the clip of her anger as she bit off the words raking against her conscience. It wasn't Halva's fault. It never had been.

"That's true enough, but I never said I wasn't going to trade with you."

"If you won't take me with you, then it's the Fleet."

"Or marriage."

She scoffed, incapable of finding the words to make this daft, impossible man understand just how deeply she chafed at the very idea.

"Here, now." He slipped the atlas into an empty satchel at his side and grabbed a leather cord tied around his neck. He hauled up on it, a round, silverish disk dangling from its end. Slipping the cord over his neck, he tossed it to her.

Silka snatched it from the air on instinct and cradled the silver disc in one hand. Under closer inspection, she marked it as real silver—even if it were blemished by time and sweat. The face was a fine piece of work, a perfect representation of the lunar calendar engraved all around it. The great fat red moon dominated most of the depiction, but its silver little sister made her appearance in the chronology of the sky, too—rising up to cause the monsoon season. A banner had been engraved across the top curve, words in old imperial in all capitals.

She sucked air through her teeth when she recognized it. "This is a veteran's shield. From the Catari war."

"Mine, specifically. Won by service. Kept the ships in the air, I did." He glanced over his shoulder toward the edge of the garden, but Silka couldn't parse the meaning in the motion.

She flipped it over and saw on its back the small, circled mark of what must have been his family's crest. The symbols were meaningless to her, she'd never given a whit for noblebone politics, but she suspected they were indicative of an older line. It was a very simple design, the symbols not yet cluttered by time and the proliferation of families who could afford such a mark. His first name was carved just below it. Family Mark—Tibal.

"What family?" she asked.

He clucked his tongue against his teeth. "That can't be the most interesting thing you see there."

Silka looked again. Her mouth slipped open of its own accord.

All around the back rim of the disc—where notches should have been carved by the Valathean depositories each time he went to make a withdrawal against his veteran's stipend—the metal was naked. Blank. Four years the Catari war had been over, and Tibal hadn't drawn his stipend. Not even once.

"That's... a lot."

"Enough to keep a young lady independent for a few years until she finds her feet."

Her head snapped up so fast a kink spasmed in her neck. She stared at him, mouth still open, trying to puzzle out the meaning behind the glimmer in his eye. "You can't be serious. It's a fortune."

"It's blood money, to me. I don't want it—so it might as well do some good. You keep that." He dragged a dog-eared sketchpad from his satchel and tore out a page, then scribbled something quick in charcoal. "Take these numbers and the shield to any Valathean counting house. They'll give you what I'm owed. It won't be luxury, mind, but it'll be enough."

She took the slip of paper, unable to hide the tremble in her fingers, and stared at the string of neat numbers. His personal cipher. The key to his treasure chest.

"Won't they wonder who I am?"

He grinned. "Tell 'em you're the missus. Can't argue with that."

She snort-laughed. "Marriage or the Fleet..."

"Marriage is looking brighter, eh?"

She closed the distance between them and pressed a kiss against his cheek. The muscle of his jaw clenched, startled, and he took a half-step back, bringing a hand up to cover the spot. He tasted of sour sweat and old grime—and something a little deeper. A tinge of musk.

"Now, there's no need for that, it's only on paper, you know."

"I know." She winked, just to watch the knot of his throat bob as he swallowed.

"And so now I'm misses..." She glanced back at the family mark, something itchingly familiar in its stark lines. "Mrs. Tibal? They might expect me to know my new family name at the counting house, you know."

A subtle cringe rippled through the muscles of his shoulders, and he ducked his head, glancing from side to side. "I suppose." He reached out and took the paper back, scrawled his name across it and passed it back to her.

She chewed her lip, brow raised. "You're a—"

"Hush, now."

"It's just that... I thought—"

"Illegitimate, and far removed at that." He tapped the back of his neck. "No brand."

"I see. Does he know?"

"I don't talk about it."

Laughter rolled out from the sitting room, making them both jump. Guilt reared its head in Silka's heart and she wrinkled her nose in thought. "Nevermind that. Can you get the book on Detan? It's important he be the one—"

"Easy, missus, I've been doing this awhile now. And I think, that between us, things just might work out for our bumbling companions after all."

He plucked one of Halva's fruits from the vine, then dug the atlas out and offered it back to her. "Deal?"

Silka grinned. "Deal."

She took the atlas from her new husband and hid it once more under her shawl. Her steps felt lighter, her smile came easier, and her grin was quick as she walked back toward the sitting room, intent on her target. If they wouldn't come to her, well then, she'd just have to go to them.

It came rather as a shock to Silka Yent to discover she was having fun.

19

Warden Faud, Detan was coming to discover, had heard of him. He was a big man, half a head taller than Detan and barrel-shouldered, his wide, flat face set with eyes the color of old milk. Detan half suspected the aging Warden couldn't see a hand in front of his face, but he was doing a rather fine job of giving Detan the stink-eye regardless.

"So." Faud pursed his lips around the word. "What brings a man like you to my city?"

Detan was not at all surprised to hear the subtle emphasis behind *like you*, and imagined he could feel the venomous sting those words held.

"The flowers of Aransa are renowned all across the Scorched." He squeezed Halva's arm to make his meaning clear.

"Came looking for a wife, did you?" Faud pressed a honeyed millet cake into his mouth and chewed slowly, deliberately, gaze locked on Detan. Doing everything he could to unnerve him, Detan suspected. Which meant Captain Leshe had dropped a few words in his ear. Detan forced himself to smile just as big as he could.

"No, sir, that was a happy accident."

"Have a lot of accidents, do you?" Faud's words speared Detan, stunned him into silence.

Accidents. He'd had one, a long time ago. One everyone knew about—rumor traveled faster than wind on the Scorched. An explosion at the Hond Steading mines—an entire spoke of miners lost in the conflagration. All save Detan Honding. Who had, or so he let rumor tell, lost all his selium-sense to the trauma.

He swallowed. It was like trying to breathe nettles.

"Why don't we retire to the garden?" Halva said when the silence had dragged on too long for anyone's comfort.

"Pah," Faud said. "And bake alive? Tell you one thing I miss about Valathea—the shade. The sun's harsh as the grave on this continent."

A distressed wrinkle wormed its way across Halva's brow. There was something at play here he couldn't see, and that was rankling his calm something fierce. While Halva went on babbling pleasantries at Faud, Detan scraped his gaze over the small crowd gathered in the sitting room.

Those rag-swathed miscreants that Halva claimed were her guests huddled around the small sampling of food set out, arguing over the providence of a piece of cheese. Though Detan didn't much mind the presence of scoundrels in general—he counted himself amongst them—these made his skin prick with unease.

He remembered the second face on the flier, belonging to a man he did not recognize from the mugging. These could be guests of Halva's, as she claimed, but they could also be agents of his harassers. Either way, he wasn't the only one they were making uncomfortable. Lord Erst kept glancing their way as if they were rockvipers coiled to strike.

Just when Detan felt like he was about to peel out of his own skin from anxiety, Tibs appeared amongst the unfriendly faces of the sitting room, that martial-looking woman Detan had spotted in the Blasted Rock at his side. Each wore a pleased smile. Detan could only hope Tibs had done them some good on his investigation of the Erst abode.

"Evening, Warden," Tibs said as he floated up alongside Detan. "How fares fine Aransa?"

Faud eyed him through slitted lids, fingers frozen halfway to depositing some morsel in his mouth. "Very well, young man. Though I had a disturbing talk with my watch-captain this morning."

"Oh?" Tibs asked, all polite interest.

"Indeed. It appears an influx of false grains have been rolling—well, bumbling—around Aransa lately. Never seen the like before. She has assured me that the problem will be cleared up shortly. A few days, at most."

"Your Watch-captain must be very good to suss out a new problem so quickly," Detan said, unable to hide a slight catch in his throat. He covered the noise by taking a sip of his water.

"There's no finer in all the Scorched." He sighed at the sad millet cake clutched between his fingers. "If only the food here were so fine."

Detan was surprised to feel Halva tense and lean forward beside him. Before she could speak, Tibs produced a strange little fruit from his pocket. It filled his whole hand, and was covered in bruise-purple skin with fine, downy spines.

"Give this a try." Tibs sectioned off a wedge of the fruit with his meatknife and passed it over to Faud. The flesh was dark pink, verging on red, and the whole thing gave off a vaguely sweet aroma.

Faud sniffed at it and frowned. "What is it?"

"A type of pear, sir. A variation on the hairy empress fruit," Halva squeaked, which Detan thought was a rather odd state to be in over a piece of fruit.

With a careless shrug, Faud discarded the millet cake on a nearby table and popped the pear-thing into his mouth. He chewed. He frowned. He grinned bright enough to rival the sun.

"Now that, is marvelous. Where did you get such a thing, child? There hasn't been a Valathean mercer ship here in months—surely fresh fruit would not have kept so long."

"It's my own devising," she spoke all in a rush, hands fluttering through the air as if she could force physical shape into her words. "It grows fast, and trains well, and requires very little water. Here, let me show you."

Halva abandoned Detan's arm without a thought and took up Faud's, ushering him back toward the garden as if they'd suddenly become the only two people in all the world.

"Huh," Detan said, propping his hands on his hips.

"Maybe," Tibs said, "we should join them?"

Detan was unnerved to see a knowing glance pass between his partner and that martial woman. The woman nodded, badly hiding an amused grin, and stepped forward to take the arm Halva had deserted. A new weight settled in the oversized pocket of his tunic, pressing against still-aching bruises.

He looked down at her, but she just smiled up at him with eyes as bright as well-water. He glanced at Tibs, and only got a wry smirk.

Fine then, leave me out of the fun.

"Let us away to the gardens," he said, and strode forward with all the confidence of a man who knew exactly what he was doing.

The martial-woman, who introduced herself as Silka, steered him out amongst the fronds toward the heart of the garden. Detan recognized the little table he had sat at only the day before, beaten and weary. Where he had, according to everyone around him at any rate, proposed to Halva.

The Lady in question had a large book spread across the table, coils of hair working their way free from the bun on her head as she bent over it, her voice bright and quick as she shared botanical secrets with a surprisingly rapt Warden Faud.

Detan hadn't a clue what any of it meant but, apparently, it was fascinating stuff. He shot a pained glance at Tibs, who cleared his throat rather loudly. Silka flinched beside him and glanced over her shoulder. A few of the party-goers were trickling out, no doubt wondering what was so interesting about the garden that it had drawn out the Lord and Lady of the hour. Halva's father was amongst them, his smile faltering as he caught sight of his daughter.

"Oh, my Lord Honding, you are too funny!" Silka burst into a fit of giggles and slipped her arm free to give him a mighty thwack on the back.

"Huh?" He coughed, lurching forward a half-step as the force of Silka's blow awakened the flaring pain of his bruises.

As he staggered, her arm slipped down and gave his pocket a little nudge. Subtle, practiced. He was just as surprised as anyone to see a great leather-bound book tumble out and land with an echoing thump against the stone-laid path.

It was, quite possibly, the biggest book he'd ever seen. Its cover was tooled with the Ersts' name and family crest, the landmasses of the known world splayed out beneath it all. Their atlas. The atlas of a family of famous diviners.

Detan swallowed. Well, Auntie Honding was certainly not going to be disappointed with this gift.

The thunk of leather on stone drew every eye gathered. Halva stared, open-mouthed with real shock. Had she not known what her friend was up to?

Of course not. Silka was keeping her spirit-sister from marrying an idiot. At any cost.

Warden Faud was the first to find his tongue. "Thief!"

The effect, Detan was pleased to discover, was chaos. Someone took up a shriek in the back of the garden, drowning out whatever it was Halva was yelling at him. Silka, that caverat, feigned terror and darted away, running smack into a few of the men of the crowd rushing forward to apprehend Tibs and Detan.

Heart pounding in his ears, Detan scooped up the atlas and shoved it back in his pocket, then bolted for the back wall of the garden. Tibs fell in beside him, and then the world went sideways.

The air rushed out of him as he slammed into the ground, and after an experimental wiggle he discovered one of the beggar women wrapped around his legs, fingers fumbling for his pockets.

She bit down on his arm, and he squealed as he twisted and kicked out. His heel caught her in the knee, bearing down on the bony knob, and she screeched rage and pain as Tibs grabbed Detan by the arms and hauled him free.

"Catch him, you cowards!" Faud bellowed above the chaos. "I will have the mad bastard flayed and made into a sail for my ship!"

"That seems excessive!" Detan yelled.

"Just run, sirra!"

The party-goers had gotten something like organized, and a half dozen boot steps came pounding down the path in their general direction. Detan swore, cursing his bruised body and his winded lungs. Cursing the damned thorn-ridden shrubs Halva had planted near the edge.

Detan thrashed his way through the offensive vegetation until he struck the adobe wall marking the level edge. With a boost from Tibs he scrambled to the top, then reached down and gave Tibs a hand-up beside him.

They stood there, at the top of the wall, two targets clear as day against the blue Aransan sky, and waved back to their pursuers.

"Thanks for your hospitality!" Detan called out.

Rocks pinged off his arms, pelted against the mud-and-stone wall.

"You've nowhere to go!" Faud yelled back.

Detan grinned at him. Grinned at Tibs. Grinned down at their pursuers, now making their way through the same thorny mess of shrubbery. And then he spun and jumped off, into the sky beyond.

Cries of alarm sounded behind him, but he thunked against the deck of his flier with little more than a sore ankle. Tibs landed in a light crouch beside him, annoyingly hale. He didn't have a single scratch on him.

"How'd you dodge the thorns?" Detan asked.

"Let you go first."

He groaned and rolled his eyes, then leapt across the deck and severed the long rope holding their flier in place. It drifted away from the wall immediately, pushed by the gentle breeze of Aransa. Detan paid the drifting ship no mind as Tibs rushed to the helm and grabbed hold of the primary wheel. The ship's drifting halted, and Tibs let the stabilizing side wings out a little to ease the subtle sway of the deck.

Rocks scattered about Detan's feet, pinged off his arms and head. "Hey!"

Faud's red-flushed face appeared over the wall, rounded fingers gripping tight to the top of it. "Do not return to Aransa, you hear? Show your face in this city again and I *will* tan your hide and make a sail of it!"

"Message received!" He snapped a salute, and the Warden spat over the wall in response. Lovely.

Tibs took them out of rock-throwing range and Detan joined him on the cranks that turned the flier's downward-facing propellers, urging the ship to a height above the garden. Selium-craft had their own natural, neutral buoyancy depending upon the weight of the ship, its cargo, and how much sel was crammed in it, but selium was always eager to lift, and the slightest nudge upward could overcome that neutral plane.

Without either the aid of the propellers, or the attention of a sel-sensitive moving the sel, the ship would drift back down over time, but that was all right. He and Tibs were pretty good with the cranks, after all. Detan was always loathe to give anyone the idea that he still had any of his sel-sense left. He wasn't about to blatantly manipulate it in front of all these witnesses.

As they drifted up, Detan abandoned his post and scrambled back over to see how things were getting along in Halva's garden.

Chaos, it seemed, was unwilling to loosen its grip.

Those who had chased them to the edge of the garden had turned back toward its heart, but they'd only discovered further trouble in the manner of two pissed off beggar-women. Or muggers. Whatever they were, they were working up a storm of trouble. To his deep dismay, he saw his own harassers had arrived, free of the ties they'd left them in. Detan grimaced. Must have taken them all night and morning to sneak their way up to Halva's level, but they'd done it, and looked mighty upset they'd missed his appearance at the party.

Tables were knocked over. Gallant men whose worst experiences with pain had been getting belted as boys tried to subdue the terrors, but it was no use. In the middle of it all Halva and Silka stood, back to back, the botany book clutched tight against Halva's chest and a cheese knife clutched tighter in Silka's fist.

"I feel we should do something," Detan said as the shadow of Tibs fell over his shoulder.

"We do have a Watcher to hand."

Detan frowned down at the tumult below and heaved a sigh great enough to send spirals of pain lancing out from his abused ribs. "I suppose we do have to let him out eventually."

He turned and adjusted his tunic, feeling the selium balloon Tibs had given him what felt like ages ago now. He'd been subduing it subconsciously, holding the cupful of it steady in his mind. Now that he made himself actively aware of it he could feel it tugging at him, desiring nothing more than to fly away.

A small thing, that giant's fistful of sel. But enough, perhaps, to ease the fall of a man from a height. A height safely away from spear prods and thrown rocks. Detan winked at Tibs, relishing the confusion wrinkling the man's forehead, and strode forward with newfound confidence of his own. He wrenched open the trapdoor and was slammed in the chest by a barreling Watcher.

"Urgh!" His back slapped the deck and once more all the air escaped him, white stars of pain dancing before his darkened eyes.

He heard Tibs say something, the words themselves lost to the ringing in his ears, and then the great weight was heaved off his chest and air returned to him. Gasping, he levered himself to his feet and leaned forward, hands propped on his knees. That cursed Watcher stood between him and Tibs, baton wavering as he tried to decide which one of them he'd more enjoy bashing.

"Peace," Tibs said, "we don't mean you any harm."

"You are *both* under arrest! For counterfeiting coinage and imprisoning a watcher of Aransa. Kneel on the deck of the ship so that I may properly restrain you."

Detan shared a look with Tibs. It was difficult not to laugh.

"I understand your position," Detan said. "Really, I do. You spent a rough night and I'm sorry for it, but we didn't set you free just to go on a nice little walk back to the station house. The Erst family home is under attack, and requires your assistance."

His eyes narrowed. "You're lying."

"See for yourself." Detan gestured toward the forward rail and lifted both his hands into the air, palms forward, to show they were empty of any weapons.

Banch half scuttled, half walked to the rail, never taking his eyes from them and never once letting his baton drop. As he reached the edge he bent his knees to be ready to spring away and braced one hand on the rail. Detan rolled his eyes.

"Just look, won't you?"

Banch peered over the edge, and swore some rather un-Watcher-like words. "What did you do?"

"Me?" Detan threw his arms in the air. "I didn't do a pitsdamn thing. Whatever that is happened after I'd left."

"*Right* after?"

"I'm sure I don't know what you're implying. Are you going to help those people, or not?"

"Of course I am! Take this ship down so that I can disembark, then kneel in the manner I directed."

Detan snorted. "Not going to happen. I'm not bringing my flier anywhere near that madness, and I'm sure as shit not kneeling down for you."

The muscles of Banch's neck strained so that Detan feared the man would burst. "Then how do you expect me to help them, *Lord* Honding."

"Funny you should ask." Detan pulled the balloon from under his tunic and held it out. "This should be enough to break you fall."

"You can't be serious."

"Better hurry. Sounds like a real disaster down there."

Banch tapped the baton against an open palm. "I could force you—"

"No," Tibs said in the hardest voice Detan had ever heard him muster, "you couldn't."

The knot of Banch's throat bobbed once, twice, and then he threw his hands in the air and tucked the baton away. "Fine, give me the blasted thing. But if you ever set foot in Aransa again—"

"So we've been told." Detan looped the little ball of sel around Banch's wrist and cut the metal weights free. "Best hold onto that with two hands."

With Tibs and Detan ushering him forward, Banch approached the edge of the flier and peered down into the chaos in the garden. He put one foot up on the rail, then spared a glance back at Detan. "I don't suppose I could entreat upon your sense of mercy to bring the ship lower?"

"Fresh outta' mercy. You'll be fine. Unless you weigh considerably more than I've guessed."

The watcher swallowed, self-consciously adjusting his weapons belt, then heaved himself into a sitting position upon the rail. His feet dangled over the empty air, and he leaned forward as if testing the waters of a very hot bath.

"On with it." Tibs gave the watcher a shove.

With a startled yelp Banch tipped over, flailing to get both his hands on the balloon string. Detan rushed forward and gripped the rail, peering down at the dark blue blob as it slalomed gently on the faint breeze.

"Huh, it worked," Detan said.

"Had your doubts?" Tibs asked.

"A wise man is never certain."

"Lucky us we're blessed with your sagacity, then."

Detan snorted as cries of alarm began to rise up from the party goers. He pushed away from the rail and strode back towards the helm, not wishing to see what would happen next. He'd done what he could, and felt certain that if he were to stay any longer it would only make matters worse.

As he took up the primary wheel he felt an urge to reach out with his sel-sense, to feel the great buoyancy sacks suspended above the deck and guide the flier through the skies by the force of his whim, not the strength of his arms. But he was too close to the city yet, and any hint of sel-ability might make him a more hunted man than he already was.

Selium-sensitives worked selium mines. He'd done that.

Once.

Tibal slid up beside him, hands folded behind his back. Detan had no doubt in his mind that Tibs was the better pilot—the better man all around, if he were being real honest—but still he clung to the wheel, turning the flier's back on the sweep of Aransa.

Tibs let him, stifling any complaint. Both of them holding back on any words at all until they were well out over the empty scrubland and sands.

"I hope," Detan said, "she won't be too upset by my abandonment."

"Something tells me she'll be fine."

Tibs pulled that strange fruit he'd shared with Faud out of his pocket and sliced off another chunk, chewing it over with care. Detan eyed it, suspicious.

"Seems strange, her wanting to use the Honding name just to get an audience with the Warden."

"Her family was having some trouble fulfilling an old concordant. I doubt her father was keen on a change." Tibs chewed noisily.

"Wonder if she was ever interested in marriage at all." Detan cursed himself for the traitorous hint of wistfulness creeping into his voice.

"I imagine she was," Tibs said, his tone perfectly flat.

"Wonder if she'll ever forgive me."

"I imagine she will."

Detan glanced sideways at his old friend and saw a tell-tale crook to the corner of his fruit-smeared lips. "You seem mighty knowledgeable of the Lady's proclivities."

Tibs smirked. "I had a rather illuminating conversation with my wife."

"Your *what?*" Detan jumped, jerking the wheel so that he had to scramble to get the flier laid out straight again.

"You met her. Miss Silka Yent, the martial woman."

"You didn't—I mean, how? When?"

He shrugged and tossed the stone of the fruit over the side of the ship. "Wasn't nothing romantic. She was in a hard place—marriage, the Fleet, or poverty. Didn't have any suitors in particular in mind, so—"

"So you offered yourself?"

"Seemed, after all that trouble, that somebody should be getting married."

"I see." Detan laughed, a wild and frantic sound. "So, no more blood money, then. At least somebody will be relieving the counting houses of it."

"My thoughts exactly."

Detan shot Tibs a scowl, but he just wiped the fruit stain from his lips on the back of his sleeve and wandered off to see to the fitting on one of the fans, leaving him alone with his thoughts. And the book. With a weary grunt he chocked the wheel, heading straight northeast toward Hond Steading, and dragged a crate over on which to sit. The atlas he pulled out and laid in his lap, flipping through decades of family history—of exploration. It was a singular work, and Auntie Honding would be right proud to own it.

And if she didn't, he might just push her off the flier with a selium balloon of her own.

20

Halva sat on the balcony of her father's home, sipping tea through bruised lips. The sun dusted a sunny beam across her table, warming the stiff ache that had crept into her muscles and joints. While the bulk of the party's turmoil had avoided her, she still felt its aftereffects in the tightness of her back and the sore complaint of her feet.

A mild annoyance, truly, to have gained everything she desired.

Silka lounged across from her, the cross-stitch hoop she had been laboring over the past half moonturn forgotten. Her friend bore the purpling bruises of battle, as she'd happily jumped into the fray, but she wore them with languid contentment, cat-like pride.

"I think," Halva said into the stretching silence, "that things might have gotten out of hand."

"Really?" Silka drawled, "I hadn't noticed."

Halva grunted a laugh, a soft sting radiating from her mouth. The bruising of her lips she treasured, pressing the rim of her teacup against them to spread the slight pain deeper. Those she had earned from her lover's lips.

"Well," Silka pressed, "is it done?"

Halva gave her friend a coy smile over the rim of her teacup. "There are so very many things to which you might be referring. I hardly know where to begin."

"Then begin with the pears."

"Ah, yes." She felt her grin twitch, growing sly without her permission. "Daddy and Faud stayed up well into the night, drinking brandy and comparing scrapes from the kerfuffle. Like two great, old war buddies come together to compare scars. They have become, I fear, the best of friends. And the good Warden has made certain to draw up and have signed all the paperwork appropriate for a new family concordant."

"Hah!" Silka clapped her hands in delight. "I knew the Warden wouldn't be able to resist once he'd had a taste. The Botanist Lady Erst. I think it rather suits you."

"As do I." She grinned, popping a leftover millet cake into her mouth.

"And the other?"

"Hmmm?"

"Don't tease. If you are to be married in truth then I must have a dress for the occasion—and so it's best you warn me now, so that I will have the time to figure out how to purchase one."

She nearly choked on her cake. "You would wear a dress, for me?"

"Of course I would, ninny. Now go on, spill."

A flush crept its way to Halva's cheeks as she wiped the sticky honey from the cake clean on a small napkin. The memories were all still so very fresh, so very personal. And yet, she knew there would never be a day in which she could recall them without a blush.

"Cranston was lingering nearby, of course. And while daddy was busy with Faud, well, we... Talked. He was so very sweet, Silkie. He promised to wait, no matter how long it took."

"And? How long should it take?"

Halva grasped the new silver chain that hung round her neck and pulled it out, revealing the gold band dangling from the end of it. Plain as it was, it was the most precious thing in the world to her.

"Daddy insists we wait a respectable amount of time after ending my 'engagement' with Detan, but hinted that it should be about the time our new concordant arrives."

"Wonderful!"

"And that should be enough time," she said as she slipped the engagement band back into its hiding place, "to work up some scheme for you."

"For me?" Silka's eyes went wide with feigned ignorance. "Whatever do you mean?"

"Do you think me blind to your troubles? I have been thinking on your mother's ultimatum, marriage or the Fleet, and I wonder if—"

"Oh please, no more schemes for at least another turn of the moon. And regardless, I assure you, I've taken care of my future already."

Halva went stiff and cold all over. "You didn't."

"Didn't what?" She hid her expression behind a cup.

"You did! You signed up for the Fleet! Black skies, we can get you out of this mess. Just let me—"

"Whoa." A tiny chuckle snuck through. "I didn't do any such thing."

"But it was marriage or the Fleet..."

"Yes, and?"

"You married? When? Who!?" Halva burst forth from her chair and stood with her fists clenched, looming over Silka as if she could squeeze the information out of her with the sheer force of her presence. With a shameful grimace she sat back down and smoothed her morning dressing gown.

"It was at your party, in fact. Out in the garden. That young man your Detan was with offered me, well, his veteran's stipend, really. It's all just a marriage of paper, but it's enough to keep me independent."

Halva's mouth worked around empty air as she struggled to organize her flying thoughts into words. "Tibal? Detan's traveling companion is—is—your *husband*?"

"On paper." Silka shrugged.

"How can you be sure it's not another trick of theirs?"

"I thought of that, and I knew you'd protest, so I went to the counting house this morning to see if I could make my first withdrawal." Silka pulled a leather thong from around her neck and deposited a well-polished veteran's shield in the center of the table. Halva stared at it, disbelieving, but her shock only ran deeper as Silka produced a slim leather envelope from her robe. She sat it on the table with a tell-tale clatter.

"I can hardly believe it." Halva picked up the fine leather envelope and weighed the contents in her hand. Judging by the weight and volume they were silver—and plentiful. She couldn't recall ever having held so many grains at once before. "You're a rich woman, Mrs—?"

Silka pointed to the medallion. "Turn it over, I think you'll recognize the crest."

Halva flicked it over, and squeaked with shock at the familiar lines staring up at her. "Well then. What will you do now?"

A little grin crept its way across Silka's features. "I'm considering mounting an expedition to explore the midlands of the Scorched. An event, perhaps, wherein one might require the keen eye of a botanist?"

Halva felt her lips contort to mirror Silka's grin. "I just might know someone."

Though their cups were already half-gone, they held them up to one another and clinked a joyous toast.

"To your future, Mrs. Wels," Silka said.

"And to yours, Mrs. Honding."

The Adventures of Detan & Tibs Continue in the

Scorched Continent Trilogy

Steal the Sky

Break the Chains

Inherit the Flame

To keep updated with my latest stories, sign up for my newsletter! Here's the direct link: https://www.subscribepage.com/m6i0q2_copy2

You'll be first to hear about new releases, sales, public appearances, and you'll probably get some cute cat pictures.

You can also join me over on twitter, though I communicate mostly via gifs: https://twitter.com/MeganEOKeefe

Printed in Great Britain
by Amazon